# SUZIE EMPOWERED

## Blake Allwood

Content Warning:

This story contains an attempted rape/sexual assault scene, plus bullying and threatening behavior

Titles by Blake Allwood:

<u>Transitions Series</u>
Aiden Inspired
Suzie Empowered
Bobby Transformed

<u>By Chance Series</u>
Love By Chance (1)
Another Chance With Love (2)
Taking A Chance For Love (3)

<u>Big Bend Series</u>
Love's Legacy (1)
Love's Heirloom (2)
Love's Bequest (3)

<u>Romantic Series</u>
Romantic Renovations (1)
Romantic Rescue (2)
Romantic Recon (3)

<u>Coming Home Series</u>
Tenacious

Purchase at:
https://readerlinks.com/mybooks/4515

Join Blake's email list to get advance notice of new books

and receive his occasional newsletter:

https://www.blakeallwood.com

Thank you to the following people for their assistance:

Janet Sitzmann – Beta Reader
Amy Leibowitz – Editing
Dee Friloux – Proofreading
Valerie - Advice

2$^{nd}$ Edition

Ann Attwood - Editing

A special thank you goes to all my friends and family who supported me, I couldn't have done it without you.

And finally, an extra special thanks to my husband who continues to tolerate me, no matter how many of these rabbit holes I keep going down.

# Prologue: Suzie

Eddie McPeak pinned me against the passenger seat of his mom's Chevy. At first, I giggled as he began kissing my neck, and playfully tried pushing him away.

When he refused to budge, that was when the panic began to set in.

"Eddie, move back!" I said as forcefully as I could, letting him know I wasn't into this any longer.

He ignored me. Instead, he moved his body to trap me even more.

We were parked about two blocks from the school in a back alley, and I was dressed in lots of pink taffeta. I tried again to push Eddie off, the panic increasing when I noticed he had pulled his dick out.

He was fumbling around trying to get into my dress. Luckily, this wasn't the kind of dress that allowed for easy access, so he began to masturbate instead.

I was pissed and mortified all at the same time. God, this was rape. The motherfucker was trying to rape me.

I reached for the door handle, but Eddie recognized what I was doing and stopped me. I began hitting him, but I was too weak to stop him, so I did the only thing I could. I pretended I was interested, and when he was really into it, I carefully reached up, grasped the handle and quickly scooted out of the car. He tried to grab me, but I scrambled up and ran away screaming. A small piece of the pink fabric ripped off in his hand as I escaped.

I was terrified he was going to drive toward me, or come after me on foot. If he had, he could've easily caught me. I was in no way prepared to handle a horny teenage boy.

He must have felt guilty, or got scared, because he didn't come after me, but the damage was done. I was freaked out.

When I got to the school, I found my best friend whose tongue was locked with her boyfriend's and asked for her phone. She looked at me weird, and asked what was wrong, but I just shook my head. If I told her, I'd lose it, and I didn't want to be the geek who lost her marbles on prom night.

My mom answered in a chipper voice. "Hi, sweety, how's your night?"

"Mom, I need you to come get me. Come get me, right now!"

I stifled a sob, which must have been enough, because she was at the school in less than fifteen minutes. I knew she had sped to get to me as it usually took twice that much time to get to the school from home. When she came into the gym, one of the supervising teachers stopped her at the door; a moment later, they were both looking for me. I rushed toward my mom as soon as I saw her, and pulled her out of the gym as quick as I could. "I want to go home. I need to go home... MOM!"

Mom's face was tight with worry, and she put her arm around me, trying to look nonchalant, so I wasn't embarrassed, and pulled me toward the car that she had left running in front of the gymnasium's entrance. When we got in, I lost it. I was crying and screaming. Mom pulled away from the curb, drove to the first parking lot that was out of sight of the school, and pulled me into her arms.

"Baby, what happened?" I just shook my head. I couldn't tell her, I couldn't look her in the face, but I thought she probably already knew. "Are you okay for me to drive home?" she asked.

I still couldn't face her, but I nodded. She never took her hand off mine as we drove home, and parked the car in the garage. I heard my dad say something, assuming he had come through the garage door, but Mom must have shooed him away, because when I looked up, he was gone.

Mom helped me out of the car, and held me in a tight hug. I kept crying, sobbing, and unable to control myself. When the cries began to slow, she took me by the arm and led me into the house, where we both sat side by side on the sofa.

"Baby," she said in a soothing voice. "Tell me what happened."

I shook my head, and tears began to come out again, along with the hysteria. "I can't," I kept chanting.

Mom waited until I calmed down, and said once again, "Baby, I need you to tell me what happened. I can't help you if I don't know."

This time, I was able to make eye contact, but no words would come out.

Mom saw that I was struggling and asked, "Is this about Eddie?"

I nodded, and was surprised there were no more tears.

"Did he try to hurt you?"

I thought about that for a moment. *No, he didn't try to hurt me. He tried to fuck me.* I shook my head no.

"Did he try to have sex with you?"

My mom was always blunt when it came to sex, so I wasn't surprised she didn't beat around the bush, but I was terrified of what would happen if I admitted that he did. I sat silently, trying to figure out what I was going to say, and then Mom let me off the hook.

"That answers my question, and I'm sorry I have to ask this, but I have to. Did he rape you?"

The tears came back then, but I was able to respond, "He tried..."

I heard something fall in the next room, and I realized that my dad was listening. I looked up and the fear filled my body.

"Mom, he'll kill him."

My mother's eyes were tender toward me, but I could see the anger banked behind them. "If I don't kill him first," she said.

I was totally freaking out, of course. I was a typical teen girl, and being singled out for any reason scared the shit out of me.

"The kids will hate me," I cried.

My parents were awesome. They understood and treated me like a person, not a stupid kid, so whenever they saw my fear, despite the fact it was usually overblown teen fears, they didn't push or belittle me.

"My dearest," Mom said. "If a man tried to force himself on you, you are not the one who should be afraid of people hating you. The person who pushes himself on you, however, should be terrified. You have the right to never be pushed into something you don't want. Your body, your choice, sweetheart."

My mom had said this to me since I first started showing an interest in boys. The repeated words comforted me, and I nodded.

"We need to call the police," she said. "Don't worry. I'll be here for you through the whole process."

At that point, my dad walked in and knelt in front of me. "As will I, sweetheart. As will I."

The cops came and took my report, with a parent solidly rooted on each side of me. Of course, there was nothing they could do. Eddie had said I'd asked for it, and that he never did anything other than masturbate next to me. It ended up being his word against mine. His family was mortified though, and luckily for all of us, they quickly moved away after that.

Unfortunately, for me, the psychological damage was done. I was traumatized by the event. Despite years of therapy, from that point forward being alone with a boy was next to impossible. Luckily, I found that I had theatrical talent, and the only boys in my high school thespian club happened to be gay. So, lucky me, I learned I could have hot men around, and still feel safe.

In college, I made sure to have lots of trusted friends with me whenever we went to the bars, but I stopped dancing at straight clubs after I graduated. I went a few times for a drink with friends, but I refused to get on the dance floor. I knew I could protect myself, but I really had no interest if I didn't have to. I tended to avoid the places single women my age frequented, and the ones who went to gay bars, tended to only want to hang around gay guys. Of course, there was no judgement there, because I was the same way.

Oh, my god, gay bars! I found that they are chock full of hot, sweaty men, and not a single damned one of them wanted to fuck a woman—much less rape her. No matter how much they rubbed your boobies, they never pinched your boobs so hard they bruised them, and at the end of the day, they were more repulsed by them than they were intrigued.

With my gay friends, and the eventual coming out of my baby brother, Aiden, I was Fag Hag Extraordinaire. And I wouldn't have it any other way.

# Suzie

The music pounded louder than usual. *Good, I thought, that's what I need. Loud music to help drown out my misery.* Even the intensity of working the Broadway stage hadn't drowned it out since Aiden, my stupid brother, had found his love and left New York—correction, he left *me*!

As I walked through the door of Stages, the ultra-popular gay dance club, the crowd started chanting my stage name, "Beta! Beta! *Beta!*"

I let it draw me out of my misery as I swirled among the sexy, hot, and very gay men.

I was surprised I had the energy to move after performing on stage for three full hours, not to mention the drudgery of removing stage makeup, but I sure as hell couldn't bear going back to my empty apartment. If I did, I'd only sit and brood.

As I bumped and grinded my way around the dance floor, I began to feel whole again. This was part of my brother Aiden's and my routine. I'd be caught up in the crowd, he'd go pout, then after a while, I'd go drag him onto the dance floor. The only problem was, he had moved to fucking eastern, bumfucking Washington. Granted, he was there with one of the hottest men I'd ever met, but that was irrelevant. He was supposed to be in New York... with me!

*God, I'm so selfish.* Would I really want Aiden to be here, instead of in love with a hunky, rich rancher in a part of the world that lit him up like a candle? No, of course not, but damn if I didn't miss him. Not only was Aiden my baby brother, but since we'd both landed in New York after moving here from Kansas City, he'd become my best friend.

These thoughts were bringing me down again. Finally giving up, I was about to leave when I spotted a familiar shape on Aiden's usual bar stool. As I moved toward him, recognition sank in.

"Clay?" I asked.

As he turned and noticed me, he smiled sadly. "Oh, hi, Suzie. How are you?"

"I'm depressed," I admitted. "I miss my stupid brother. You're looking a little blue yourself."

Clay shrugged. "Yeah, kinda."

"What happened? You can tell big sis anything."

With that, Clay launched himself into my arms and began to whimper.

"Damn, Clay, what's wrong?" I asked.

"Can we go somewhere I don't have to yell?" he asked.

"Of course we can," I said, and we left the bar and headed for Aiden's and my favorite hangout.

Aiden and I had found Vinnie's Diner shortly after he moved to New York. It was awful in most respects—the food was subpar, the greasy decor hadn't been updated since the early 1980s—and it was absolutely perfect. I think we loved it so much, because it reminded us of a burger dive on the Plaza in Kansas City, a restaurant where we spent many nights as young adults.

I went to the University of Missouri in Kansas City, and Aiden, just two years younger than me, went to the Kansas City Arts Institute. Both schools were practically next door to each other, and both were less than a mile from our hangout.

Although our Kansas City haunt had significantly better food than Vinnie's, the place still made us feel a bit like we were home.

After we got seated, I put my hand over Clay's and asked what was wrong.

He sighed before he asked, "do you remember Denim?"

"Of course I do." I flashed back to the tall, dark, and handsome guy my brother and I met here at the diner a while back.

"Well, he dumped me, said I wasn't ready for a committed relationship."

I looked at Clay, shocked. "Wow, that's a first, then."

"What?" Clay responded, becoming defensive.

"Well, honey, it's usually *you* doing the dumping. I've only known you for a couple years, but I have seen the revolving door of men coming in and out of your life." Clay slumped in his seat, and the server came over to get our order.

He continued to sit like a stone statue, so I ordered him a slice of chocolate pie and a milkshake. "Don't look at me that way," I said. "You're going through the breakup mourning process. That requires sugar and lots of ice cream. Trust me, a girl knows these things."  Despite the fact that Clay was a model and I'd never seen him eat a carb since we'd met, he just sighed and nodded.

I ordered a hamburger and fries and glanced at Clay just in time to see him wince. "How can you eat all that crap and stay that thin?"

I just laughed. "Have you ever performed in a Broadway musical?" I asked. "It's like a total aerobic workout every day of your life. At this point, I could eat nothing but sugar and still keep the fat off."

"Enjoy it, cause after the crap you just ordered me, I'll have to spend another hour in the gym tomorrow, and I'll still gain weight."

"Become a dancer, that'll take it off you." I grinned.

"Uh, no," Clay said. "Every damned server in this city is a wannabe dancer. I'm happy in front of the camera, thank you very much."  Clay had been featured in several ads in the past few months. Nothing national, but just like actors and dancers, if you got *any* work in New York, you were better off than most.

"Ok, enough chitchat, spill the beans. The gorgeous man dumped your pretty ass, because he said you don't want a commitment. Why?"

Clay looked down at his hands. "You know that night you and Aiden saw us out together?"

I nodded.

"Well, we were pretty new then, and it was our first time clubbing together. Luckily, Aiden came over to us because I was being my normal flirty self and began ignoring Denim.

"Of course, I had no way of knowing back then that I'd be so stuck on him. Like I said, though, Aiden saved my ass by telling Denim he wasn't interested in me, but Denim didn't miss how my eyes were doing their usual roaming around the dance floor, and the next afternoon, he confronted me about it."

He paused, so I nodded at him to continue.

"When he asked if I was still looking for a hook-up, I went through my usual speech about not being a commitment guy, but how I didn't sleep with anyone while dating someone else. Then I gave my speech about making no promises about forever.

"He seemed to take that well, but fast forward to last week, and we're back out dancing, and this pretty little twink starts grinding on me. Well, I didn't really want to go out with the twink, but you know me. He was pretty, so I ground back on him. The next thing I know, Denim is gone... like totally gone, no goodbye, no argument, nothing, he's just gone.

"Suzie, I've never cheated on a guy in my whole life, but I've still got this reputation for being a player. I'm not a player! Players are never honest with their toys, but I make sure I am. I *never* lead people on."

I had to bite the inside of my cheek to keep from smiling. Clay was at least honest with himself about the situation, but when he'd dated Aiden, I'd been frustrated seeing him flirt with other men, when he was supposed to be with my brother.

I looked back up as he began talking again, "I tried texting Denim all week, but he's just ignored me. I told him I was only dancing, and that I would never cheat on him, but nothing. Yesterday, I went to his home and waited on the stoop until he got back. When he saw me, he actually frowned."

Clay paused a moment, catching his breath. I could tell he was really hurting about this. When he continued, I saw the tears.

"I knew he didn't want to see me, but damn, I really missed him. He did sit down next to me, though, and I began trying to explain about the twink.  Denim put his hand up to stop me and said, 'I know you weren't cheating, and I believe you when you say you don't do that.'"

Clay glanced over at me and frowned. "Then he told me he was beginning to have feelings for me, and since I wasn't the kind of guy that could commit, he wanted to stop going out."

Clay put his head in his hands, and I responded, "If you've fallen in love with him, you should tell him."

Clay's eyes got big as he shook off the sadness. "I... I never said I was in love with him."

"You didn't say it, but you are," I replied. "I hate to be the one to break this to you, Clay, but you are well over the edge and into relationship territory." Clay's face paled and caused me to belt out a laugh.

"Honey, you are the most commitment-phobic man I've ever met, and that's saying a lot, since I seem to only have commitment-phobic gay friends. So, what are you going to do?"

Clay just sat staring at me like I'd grown three heads. When the food arrived, he stared down at it, then back up at me. "I don't know what to do," he replied.

"Well, I'm going to let you in on a little secret. If you want to keep that man, you better decide *fast*, because he is *not* going to stay single for long. He is one of the most beautiful men I've ever met, and he's also beginning to show up on billboards and in local magazines. So, you and I both know it's just a matter of time before he is swept into the big league."

Clay continued to stare at the food, until I felt sorry for him.

I got up from my seat and scooted next to him, pulling him into my arms. Damn, if that didn't set him off, and the poor guy started crying like a baby. When the tears subsided, I pulled away from him, and asked, "Would you be willing to give in just a little, and admit that you'd consider a relationship with Denim if he'd give you a second chance?"

Clay nodded, and for a second he looked like a little kid who'd gotten in trouble.

I smiled at him, then asked, "Where is he right now?"

"I don't know..." Clay said still sniffling. "...probably at home, since it's after midnight."

"Ok, let's go get him and set this right." I called the server back over, and told her we needed the food to go, then I dragged my phone out and asked what Denim's number was.

Clay was hesitant to give it to me, but after getting the big sister stare-down, he handed his phone over. Denim's number popped up at the top of his directory. Assuming Denim would ignore a call from Clay's phone, I entered it into my phone and pressed call.

"Yeah, hello?" a sleepy voice answered.

"Hi, Denim, this is Suzie Fisher. We met a while back for breakfast. I'm sitting here with Clay, and he has some things he needs to tell you." I considered handing the phone over, but decided on the spur of the moment that wouldn't be enough. If Denim thought

Clay was a player, they needed to be face-to-face when he convinced him he wasn't. "We're coming over."

"Wha... what?" the sleepy voice wasn't as sleepy as it was a moment ago. "Wait, you... you can't."

"Yeah, we can, and we are. Get ready, Princess. See you in a few." I hung up, not sure whether he'd see us or not, but I'd decided to try and set this right. Besides, the drama was helping me avoid my own loneliness.

Clay was being a huge chicken, and kept trying to talk me out of going. The truth was that I didn't even know where Denim lived, so all he had to do was refuse to tell me, but as I suspected, he was so far over the edge in love that his protests were only for show. I just followed him as he led the way to the subway, then rode across town to where Denim lived.

When we arrived at his place, I whistled. "Damn, your man can afford a Brownstone in Manhattan? He's hot and rich! Go away, Clay. I've decided I want him!"

Clay playfully pushed me away, and for the first time tonight, he grinned. "He doesn't like boobage. He likes me."

I smiled at that, knowing he was beginning to come to terms with his feelings for Denim.

I pulled him up the steps to the front door, and when I pressed the doorbell, Clay looked like he was going to bolt. I turned to get ahold of him just as the door opened. I steadied Clay, turned around, and found myself staring right into a very broad and muscular chest.

When I looked up, I realized it wasn't Denim who'd answered. The man in front of me was naked from the waist up, with just a little fuzz between two beautifully formed pecs. His face looked like it had been chiseled from rock, and coated with a beard that perfectly accentuated his features. Jet-black hair drooped into mesmerizing blue eyes that seemed to hold both humor and frustration all at the same time.

To my mortification, I realized my voice had stopped working. I could honestly say up until that moment, I'd never gone gaga over the first sight of a man before, but this perfect specimen had certainly woken deeply repressed urges in me. I cleared my throat, trying to find my voice, but still it wouldn't come.

Clay looked at me, chuckled at my awkwardness, then glanced at the man, and said, "Hi, Indi, is Denim here?"

"He is, but he doesn't want to see you." That statement was enough to knock me out of whatever was causing my brain to lock up.

"Yeah, he does," I said. "He just doesn't want to admit it." The resolve that had temporarily been overshadowed by the surprise of being face-to-chest with this hot man reignited.

The man gawked at me, apparently trying to assess my involvement, then said, "Give me a minute." He shut the door, leaving the two of us standing on the stoop.

All the shock that had initially struck me when the bearded Adonis answered the door was gone, and was quickly replaced by anger.

When the man opened the door again, and began to say Denim wouldn't see us, I pushed my way past him, pulling Clay along with me.

"Denim," I yelled in no particular direction, "Get your pretty ass down here. Clay has something to tell you."

The guardian of the door was clearly shocked by my dogged determination, and probably just as shocked that I was strong enough to push past his huge, beautiful body.

By the time he regained his senses, and tried to push us back out the door, Denim walked into the room, clearly as depressed as Clay.

"Oh, for God's sake," I said in a huff. "The two of you are so pathetic." I took control of the situation and pointed to the sofa. "Both of you sit there and talk this out. Clay..." I narrowed my eyes. "...do I need to sit here to force you to tell Denim the truth about how you feel, or can you do it yourself?"

Clay's face slowly turned red. "I think he probably knows now, anyway."

"Good." I said, then turned toward the door where the Adonis still stood. "You. Muscleman," I demanded. "Give them space." As I was about to leave, I turned to the two men who were staring at each other like lost puppies who'd just found their owner. "One of you call me tomorrow and let me know how this went." Then, I was out the door.

# Indi

Denim had woken me up from a deep sleep all in a panic. "They're coming," he said, wringing his hands.

"Wha... what?" I said, rubbing the sleep out of my eyes.

"Clay. He's coming. I need your help. I need you to keep him from coming in."

I leaned up on my elbows, shaking my head at my brother. "Why can't *you* keep them from coming in?"

Denim's eyes were becoming more panicked. "I'll cave," he said. "I miss him too much, and I'll just cave in."

I shook my head, trying to get the rest of the sleep out of it as I got up, pulling on a pair of gym shorts I'd set out for the next morning. "Denim, if you have feelings for this guy, then you should tell him," I said.

"That's just the point. I did tell him, but he isn't the kind of guy that does long-term relationships. He's a player." Denim leaned back against my doorframe, the panic now accompanied by tears.

"Damn," I said, then came over to pull my little brother into a hug. "You have it bad, don't you?" I asked.

Denim just nodded against me.

I pulled back, asking, "Is there any chance you might be wrong about this guy? People who don't think they're relationship material, change every day when they meet the right person."

Denim shook his head. "Not this one. I don't think he could give up the chase, even if he wanted to."

I sighed, and followed Denim down to the kitchen. I turned the kettle on, and listened to him go on and on about how this guy was never going to be relationship material, that he was just kidding himself, and it was best if they broke it off now, before he fell any harder for him.

Of course, this wasn't the first time I'd heard all this. For the past week, Denim had been moping around the house. I'd heard him crying in his bedroom, and mumbling to himself while pacing the floor. Denim was an emotional man, so I'd seen him messed up over a guy before, but this time was pretty epic.

I'd only met Clay a couple times. He seemed nice enough to me, but then again, as Denim had told me on more than one occasion, I was straight and had the emotional capacity of a gnat. So, who was I to question him?

I chuckled to myself for a second, thinking about my relationship with Denim. He was just a couple years younger than me, but I'd always felt parental and protective of him. Mom and Dad traveled all the time. Too much, really, and the string of nannies we had growing up were anything but parental. Most of them were there for free room and board, or more probably, because they wanted to feel like one of New York's rich and famous.

Because of that, Denim and I became close in Mom and Dad's absence, and tended to lean on each other for support. He might be right though. I was straight, and maybe I didn't quite get the emotional attachment thing in the same way he did.

In fact, I probably related more to Clay in this scenario. I'd often thought being gay was probably the best thing in the world: meeting other people, and hooking up without all the emotional attachment crap that I'd had in my relationships with women, but, of course, I didn't think of guys in a sexual way. I wasn't creeped out by it or anything—hell, everyone needed someone—but not everyone wanted the same thing, right?

Of all the gay men I'd met, though, my brother was the King of emotional reactions. Oh, excuse me, *Queen*, as he often corrected me.

Denim saw me smiling and got defensive. "What? Is this funny to you?"

"Damn, little brother, stop with the drama! I was just thinking about you telling me I'm too straight to understand feelings."

Denim just nodded and smiled through his tears. "That's true, you know. You are like an emotional statue."

"Yeah, I suppose you're right. 'Course, it appears you got *all* the genetic emotions, so there's that." Denim glared at me, but couldn't help his broadening smile. He and I had argued this point more than once. I liked that he was smiling again. When he could smile, I knew he'd be okay—at least eventually.

The doorbell rang, and the panic came back into Denim's eyes. "Don't worry, I'll get rid of him," I said. Denim just nodded and disappeared into the laundry room behind the kitchen, so he couldn't be seen.

When I opened the door, I wasn't expecting a fairy sprite to be standing in front of me. The woman turned around, staring me eye-level in the chest. When she faced me, the blood literally left my head and went straight to my groin. Goddamn, she was hot!

The woman was curvy more than thin, and every ounce of her expressed confidence caused the sexual energy around her to spark like she was a walking lightning storm. Her strawberry-blonde hair framed a sassy face, with pouty lips that compelled me to lean in and taste them.

There was also something familiar about her. I had seen her somewhere before, but I couldn't quite place her. Her mouth seemed to have forgotten how to work as she looked up at me, which of course made my knees weak. I held onto the door for support, but then I heard Clay ask if Denim was here.

I heard myself say, "He's here, but he doesn't want to see you." I tried to sound convincing, but I wasn't quite able to take my eyes away from the beautiful woman in front of me. More for my own sake than theirs, I left them outside, and shut the door.

I leaned back against the wall, and took a deep breath. After recovering, I went back to where Denim was hiding, and asked him if he'd reconsider seeing Clay, but Denim was adamant he couldn't.

I came back and opened the door, but as soon as I got the words out that Denim wouldn't see them, the sprite pushed past me. The little woman packed a punch, and my body moved right out of the way, like I was a swinging door. She dragged Clay in behind her, yelled for Denim, and he came slinking out of the laundry room.

Both Clay and Denim held the same expression of longing and sadness on their faces, and it was obvious that both had shed tears. I immediately knew the sprite had been right, and these two needed to talk things out.

She sat them down on the couch like a schoolteacher in front of a couple of elementary school boys, and demanded that they talk. She even forced the playboy to admit he had feelings before she left. Of course, not in that many words, but it was clear that he did. I couldn't help but grin.

This woman was a force to be reckoned with, and all that authority radiating from her was fucking hot!.

She started to leave, then turned back my way, and ordered me to give them space, or something along those lines. She then  said for one of them to call her tomorrow and let her know how things worked out. I grinned again when the two just nodded. She went out the door, and I immediately followed.

"Hey," I said. "Wait up."

The woman stopped and turned back to me. The elementary schoolteacher expression was fading, and was being replaced with what appeared to be weariness.

"Hey, what's wrong? What you did in there was amazing," I reassured her.

She attempted to smile, but she didn't quite succeed. "I'm just tired. I had a performance tonight, and now I'm beginning to feel exhausted."

"Here, let me grab my keys and wallet, and I'll drive you home." I could see the internal conflict in her eyes.

"I can't. I don't even know you," she said. "For all I know, you could be a serial killer."

She turned to go, but I stopped her. "I'm Denim's brother, and I'll tell them I'm taking you home, so no need to be afraid. Both Clay and Denim will know I'm with you."

She glanced over at me, the exhaustion clearly getting the better of her. "Okay," she agreed, and sat down on the stoop.

When I came back out, she was leaning her head up against the railing. I could see she was tired, but clearly something else was bothering her. My car was parked just down the street, so I unlocked it and opened the passenger door for her. She smiled at the gesture and said something about chivalry not being dead. When I climbed into the driver's seat, her head was laid back on the seat.

"Okay, you have to tell me where you live." She handed her phone to me with her address and directions already plugged in, so I let it direct me to her address. She didn't live very far away, and luckily the traffic wasn't nearly as horrible as it was during the day, so we got to her home moderately fast, especially considering we were in New York.

"Are you okay?" I asked again.

She nodded, "I'm fine. Thanks for the lift."

Before she could close the door to my car, I asked, "Would you be willing to meet me for coffee or dinner sometime?"

She appeared hesitant for a moment, then shook her head. "No, that would be a bad idea." Then, she closed the door, and just like that, she was gone.

# Suzie

For one split second, I almost invited the muscled god up to my apartment, but I realized as his sexy eyes bored into me that this wasn't just one of my gay buddies—this was a man who liked women.

"No! Oh no, no, no!" my head screamed, and luckily it screamed loud enough that I listened to it.

After the Eddie incident, I was determined I would never allow myself to be in another situation where a man could overpower me again. There was a university located near my high school, and my junior year I'd toured it with a school group. We went through the gym, and they showed us the workout room. I remembered seeing a few women working out, and noticed they were as muscled up and almost as buff as the guys.

After the tour, I didn't think much more about it, but the week after Eddie, I kept thinking about how I needed to figure out how to protect myself.

One afternoon, after school, I went directly to the university's gym, and paid for a membership, which for high school's students was only ten dollars a month.

I played around with some of the equipment, but didn't really know what I was doing, then finally got the nerve to ask one of the bodybuilder women about the weights, and how to use them. The woman looked up and down my skinny frame, and I blushed. I was just about to leave, when she said, "If you're serious, I could train you." There must have been a lot of hope in my face, because when I looked at her, she smiled. "Why are you so eager to learn?" she asked.

"I have to learn," I replied, and the woman's smile faltered. I knew, even though we never talked about it, that she understood why it was so important to me.

"Let's get started then," she said, and the rest was history.

In college, I tried going to a few straight bars with my sorority sisters, but the men were disgusting, and being around them triggered my PTSD big time. I tried to get past it, but one night a very large guy reached over, and pinched my boob, so hard, it left a bruise. The anger that had come from my teenage trauma swelled up in that moment, and I punched him in the face, breaking his nose. He called me every name in the book, but I turned it back on him.

"*You don't touch without permission!*" I said, as he blinked, while blood poured down his face.

I regularly bench-pressed two hundred fifty pounds. To give you an idea what that meant, all-star Becca Swanson—MY HERO!!—could press six hundred pounds. I would never be on her level, but I was pretty good for a one-hundred-sixty-five-pound woman. All in all, the dude was lucky. I could have done a lot more damage than just his nose. Hopefully, he'd learned to keep his damn hands to himself. I knew for sure he was embarrassed for quite a while, after his frat buddies saw what I did to him.

After that, it was clear I had no business dating. I mean, sure I liked guys, but I liked them more when I could admire them from a distance.

Getting involved with a man as handsome as Denim's brother wouldn't do at all—not even a little. Men, especially those who looked like him, needed to be kept at the farthest distance possible!

# Indi

I was disappointed. I didn't even know the name of the beautiful powerhouse who had pushed me aside like I didn't even exist. It wasn't like I went for the tough girls, but I did prefer a woman who could take care of herself.

I always enjoyed participating in the arts. My talent was only ho-hum, but I loved my theatrical friends. Of course, having a gay brother who came out when we were both really young, helped me to not be afraid of hanging out with gay guys, and the women always made me laugh. I knew I was never going to be a major star, but I liked hanging with the art crowd, and later at college, I learned I liked hanging with the football players, too.

When I spoke to my career counselor, he laughed. "You've pretty much described being an agent," he said. He told me about the requirements, and convinced me a law degree was the way to go, so there I went. Six years later, I was working for Stimmen and Hensley, agent to the stars, or at least, semi-stars.

Unfortunately, I tended to only be good at recruiting friends. So, I had my brother, who was a model, a couple of his friends who convinced me to represent them, several women I knew from college who performed more chorus-line stuff than star roles, and then a handful of lead actors, who, although they had talent, had yet to hit the big time.

I was thinking about my client base, and the fact that most, if not all of them, were more friends than clients as I pulled into my parking space, in front of the brownstone my brother and I had inherited from our grandparents. That was when it struck me who the sexy woman who'd blasted her way into my home was. I said out loud to no one, "That was fucking Suzie Fisher." She had starred as the sexy diva Beta in the comedy show *Gerls*. No wonder I thought she was hot. I had lusted over her when Denim talked me into going with him to see it on his birthday.

*Gerls* was a developing cult-classic, combining bisexuality and woman-power, somewhat reminiscent of *Buffy the Vampire Slayer*. Of course, it was about the most ridiculous thing I'd ever seen, but I'd be the first to admit I laughed through most of it, and that woman who sang so beautifully, and strutted her sexy self across the stage, had left a lasting impression on me. Wow, I had her in my home, and hadn't even recognized her until now.

"That is why you don't have clients who could actually make you money," I said out loud. I shook my head as I came up to my front door. I knocked first, afraid I'd accidentally walk in on my brother and his beau. That was *not* something I ever wanted to do. When no one answered, I slipped in with my eyes closed, and hollered, "Are you two decent?" Still no comment, so I opened one eye. There was no one in the living room or kitchen, so I assumed the coast was clear.

I grabbed a glass of water from the kitchen faucet to wash down the lump in my throat that had shown up when I'd pictured Suzie in her sexy stage costume. Then, I carefully wandered upstairs. The door to my brother's room was closed, so I went to my room on the other side of the hallway, thankful I didn't hear anything as I walked by. I was happy my brother and his man had hooked back up, but I'd be damned if I wanted to hear confirmation of it!

Sleep overtook me almost immediately, and I slept right through my alarm the next morning. Damn, I had planned to get in some reps today before going to work. *Guess I'll be doing those tonight,* I sighed with acceptance. As I walked downstairs, Denim and Clay were wrapped up into each other on the couch.

"You two get a room," I said, as gruff as I could.

Denim knew me better than any other human on the planet, and therefore didn't budge. Instead, he smiled at me. "So, you took Suzie home last night. I didn't expect you here this morning."

"Nope, she shot me down," I said.

Both Clay and Denim laughed, and Clay said, "Don't feel bad. The woman is notorious for keeping men at bay. She's secretly known as the sluttiest virgin in New York. But, of course, that's only in the gay community. As far as the rest of the world is concerned, she's just a slut."

"Regardless of what people say about her, the woman can sing," I said, with a little admiration leaking from my voice before I could hide it.

"Does someone have a crush?" Denim asked, teasing me.

I told him to shut up, but I wasn't doing a very good job hiding my emotions this morning, and the smile slipped past me before I could stop it.

"Hey, why don't you join us on a double date?" Clay asked.

I shrugged, and said, "'Cause, she already said no. In fact, her exact words were, 'That would be a bad idea.'"

"That doesn't mean she doesn't like you," Clay argued.

"And we do owe her for butting into *our* love life," Denim said.

"Sure," I agreed. "Provided she's willing to come out with us, I'm game." Then, I walked back upstairs to get dressed and head to work. Little did I know that my brother and his new man were playing full-out matchmaker in my kitchen.

# Suzie

The phone rang at exactly 10 a.m., and I was still sound asleep. I shouldn't have gone out last night, and I sure as hell shouldn't have stayed out fixing two drama queens' love life. I put my hand to my head and leaned up.

"Yeah," I answered the phone, hoping to demonstrate that calling me before noon was never a good idea.

"Hey, Suzie, It's Clay."

"Oh, hi, Clay," I managed to say with at least a little grace.

"You wanted us to call and let you know how things went last night."

I was smiling, despite the fact my eyes had yet to focus. "So, how'd it go?" I asked, already knowing the answer.

"Well, I'll spare you the intimate details, but we owe you dinner. Are you off tonight?"

"No, I have a rehearsal tonight, but I should be done by eight. Is that too late?"

"Nope," he said. "That'll be perfect. Want us to pick you up?"

"Sure," I said, perplexed why someone would pick me up. "You sure you don't want me to just meet you somewhere?" I asked.

"Nope, we've got something special planned. Dress pretty," he said, and was off the line.

I realized we hadn't set a time, and Clay was being mysterious, so I was assuming he had something naughty up his sleeve. I texted him and said, *"I can be back at my place by 8:30. Pick me up around nine so I can shower and change."*

*"That works,"* Clay texted. *"See you at nine."*

I yawned and stretched. Gay boys were so silly. They probably wanted to take me to some drag show, and thought I wouldn't come if they told me. Hell, I basically was a drag queen in my role as Beta. I wasn't sure what they were so worried about. I stumbled out of my bed, mumbling to myself that there was no use trying to get back to sleep now, then turned my coffee machine on, before heading to the shower.

After my short, but hot, shower, I came back out, grabbed my phone, and texted my brother in Washington State to see what he was doing. *"Are you up yet? Oh, wait, you're on a damn ranch in the middle of hell. Of course, you're up. I bet you already shoveled shit this morning."* A few seconds later, a middle finger emoji flashed across my screen, and I was ready to get my day started. There was nothing more gratifying than pissing off a sibling first thing in the morning.

After downing my coffee, I decided I was a bit dehydrated from last night's semi-party, so I downed another sixteen ounces of water, before grabbing my gym bag. The temperature was still a little cool, which wasn't unusual in early spring, so I decided to wear my workout clothes under my sweats. I loved that my gym was only six blocks from my house. By the time I jogged there, I was warmed up and ready for my workout.

When I came in, Donna, the new front-desk person, greeted me with a smile. "Hello, Ms. Fisher."

"Hi, Donna," I responded, and reminded her for the hundredth time she didn't have to call me Ms. Fisher. I knew she probably wasn't even twenty yet, but that didn't mean she had to pretend like I was some old woman.

I ditched the sweats, and threw them in my locker, then walked out toward one of the machines. As usual, I scanned the room to see who was there. I didn't see the regulars that I was used to, but that wasn't a surprise. I tended to sleep until noonish, so I seldom got here this early. As I scanned the area, my eyes settled on the rowing machine, and damn, if I didn't look right into the bright, blue eyes of Denim's brother—the  very guy who'd taken me home the night before.

"Well, shit." Too late to get away now, and I was never a coward, even though I sure wished I could've disappeared into the wall right then. I walked over to the man, whose name escaped me, and held out a hand. He grabbed it, then apologized for being sweaty.

"No need to apologize." I shrugged. "It's a gym. Getting sweaty is the reason we're here."

"Is this *your* gym?" the guy asked.

"Yep, I'm here at least six days a week. Can't say I've ever seen you here before, though."

"It's possible we missed each other," he said. "We didn't really know each other until last night."

I didn't want to argue with the guy, or I'd have told him I knew every person who'd been here when I had, and I definitely would not have forgotten him, but what would be the point?  "Is this when you usually work out?"

He laughed. "No. I didn't hear my alarm this morning, so I woke up late. I was headed into work when I got a call from my boss that they had to shut the office down due to some gas leak. So, I took advantage of the time to get my workout done now. Is this your regular time?"

I shook my head as I was beginning to stretch. "I don't usually get here until afternoon."

"That's probably why we haven't run into each other. I'm here early, and you are... not," he said, but not before a little judgment slipped out of his mouth.

I just cocked an eyebrow, and excused myself. I really wanted to get my workout done, and have a few hours to relax before I had to be back at the theater for warm-up.

I could feel those sexy eyes watch me leave, the heat from them warming my skin as I wandered away. This guy was definitely one to be avoided. I didn't usually feel very attracted to the big bodybuilder types, but he was different. The muscles sculpted his body in a beautiful way. You could tell he trained hard, but he didn't have the typical bubble-ball muscles I was used to seeing at this gym. Yep, he was certainly sexy as hell. *Too bad he isn't gay*, I thought, before I caught myself. That was a little twisted, even for me. I shook it off, finished stretching, and began my workout.

An hour later, I'd forgotten about the hot man in the corner, and lost track of him. I guessed he'd gone, but as I was benching, he wandered over.

"Damn, that's impressive," he said, as I benched one hundred eighty pounds.

"That ain't nothing," I replied, after setting the barbell back on the frame.

The guy that was spotting me grinned. He had been my trainer for at least a year, and he was proud of my accomplishments. I told him I was done for the day, and turned back to the hunk in front of me. "I can get up to two-fifty, but I don't do that much when I'm going in for a rehearsal, or have a show. I don't want to be wobbly while on the stage.

The guy's eyes lit up, as he asked, "Really?"

"I've been weight training for years, but yeah, I've done it."

"I'm impressed," he said. "Hell, I thought you were impressive on the stage, but benching two-fifty when you're that size? Now I'm really impressed."

Before I could help myself, I was smiling. When people recognized me, they immediately went for the "can you give me something"—a photo op, an autograph—but men especially usually didn't pay much attention to my weight accomplishment. The compliment both flattered and embarrassed me.

"How long have you been working out?" I asked him, trying to take the spotlight off myself.

"I started in college," he replied. "I was a skinny geek, who had the coordination of a dizzy octopus." He chuckled. "I started working out, thinking one day I could be one of the mega bodybuilders I saw in the Olympics."

I cocked an eyebrow, looked at his very well-toned body, and said, "I don't think you made it."

He smiled. "No. I quickly realized my limit was no more than one to two hours a day. I can't really dedicate the eight hours it would take to build up to that level of mass."

"Yeah, some of us have to work," I interjected, and he nodded in agreement.

"Well, that was my last rep," I said. "Time to shower, and then head to that job we were just talking about."

"Hey," he said awkwardly, stopping me before I got away. "I know you said it's a bad idea, but what about a quick coffee before you go to work?"

I smiled, and lied about time constraints, even though I had at least three hours to kill before I had to be at the theater. "No, I'm sorry. I have just enough time to get a shower and then get to work. Raincheck maybe."

I could have kicked myself for not just saying no. Rainchecks meant there was a chance, and I had never given any guy a chance, at least not a straight one. I rushed through my shower, and darted out the front door of the gym before I could see him again. I made a quick mental note to myself, never to come to the gym before noon ever again.

# Indi

She was totally not into me. I knew it, and yet, I hoped. I had enough women friends to know that if I pushed her any further, I'd be one of those asshole men who couldn't accept no for an answer.

That was never going to be me. *Read the signals*, I said to myself. I saw her dart out of the gym, and then I felt like an even bigger loser. Shit, this whole double-date thing wasn't going to work. I'd tell Denim to call it off. If she was running to get away from me, well...

Maybe I was reading too much into this. If she was really in a hurry, she'd rush out, right? What was I doing? Leave the woman alone. She said no. That is that.

I waited a few minutes, giving her enough time to get a head start, then went toward my favorite after-workout café down the street for a cup of coffee.

Unfortunately, shit being my luck, as I walked up to the café, she was standing in an impossibly long line. I immediately thought, *Nope, she's not into me, and she was running out the door to avoid me. That's a big, fat, not interested, dude.* All the insecurities that had plagued me throughout my high school years washed over me again, and I realized no amount of bodywork was ever going to change my inner geek. I slipped away from the café before she noticed I was there.

I had another few hours to kill before I had to be back at work, so I decided to catch up on some chores that needed doing at home. Luckily, Denim and Clay were gone when I got back, so I had the house to myself. I went through some old mail, which was mostly junk, and then paid a few bills, before I slipped upstairs to grab a quick nap.

The phone woke me, and I looked at the time, realizing I'd only just fallen asleep. "Hello," I answered, still half asleep.

"Hey, where are you?" I recognized the voice of my assistant.

"I'm still at home. Why?"

"Mr. Rubin is here. He is asking for you. "

"Shit," I said. "Put me on hold, and ask if he wants to meet me for coffee."

When she came back on the line, her voice was quiet. "No, he is pissed about something. He said he wants to move his daughter to another agent."

"That's great news," I said sarcastically. "Tell him I'll be right there." I hung up, then threw my phone down on the bed, and rushed to the mirror to make sure my hair wasn't standing up on end, which it was, of course. I forced it down with some gel that Denim said I needed to use, and managed to look halfway presentable. I threw on my suit, and jogged the two blocks to work. When I came in, Mr. Rubin was the color of his red shirt."

"Mr. Rubin," I asked. "What's wrong?"

"My daughter is not going to work for that jerk one more day." Mr. Rubin was the father of Crystal Rubin, a dancer in *Hello Kissy*, an off-Broadway musical that was beginning to get a little coverage. My contract was officially with Crystal, but both she and her dad had made it clear that what he said went. So, I escorted the man into my office and shut the door.

"That man made a pass at Crystal, and now he won't let her move up and out of the chorus line, because she said no."

"Did Crystal tell you this?" I asked, immediately suspicious.

The man looked sheepish, and wouldn't make eye contact with me. "No, one of her friends told me."

"I see," I said. And, I did. "Mr. Rubin, I know Joel Silverstein personally, and I know he wouldn't put the moves on your daughter."

The man across from me stiffened. "You're going to take up for him?" he accused.

"Yeah, I am. It's no secret that Joel is gay. Like *really* gay. If it was your son we were talking about, I'd be concerned, but Crystal is about as safe as she can be."

The man across from me seemed to relax, and leaned back in his chair. "I know you think I'm overreacting. Hell, everyone thinks I'm some helicopter dad who can't let Crystal live her own life, but I know what happens to women in this town, in this business. She's only nineteen, and I can't stand the thought of her being taken advantage of."

I smiled at him, and said, "Tell me who told you." He shook his head, like he didn't want to tell me, so I asked, "Was it Tiffany Leister?" His eyes got big at the guess, which caused me to laugh.

"I think I know what's really going on. Crystal and Tiffany are competing for the same part. One of the lead actresses got sick and had to leave the show, and Joel has decided to give the part to either your daughter or her. I'm not sure how she got wind of it, as it's supposed to be a secret, but clearly, Tiffany was hoping you'd stir the mud, so she'd get the part."

"Well, that sneaky little vixen," he said. Then there was a string of Spanish, most of which I didn't understand, and the parts I did understand I chose not to acknowledge.

I went over and put my hand on the shoulder of the smaller man. "Listen, this is show business. It's brutal, but you did the right thing coming to me before going to Joel. Let's make a pact that you will do that from now on. The girls know you love Crystal, and if they can get you to embarrass her, they will, especially if they think she's a threat."

Mr. Rubin thought for a moment, then smiled. "She is a threat, isn't she? She has so much talent—like her mama did, rest her soul."

"I'd have loved to meet the great Eliza Rubin. I heard she was something impressive to see." The man shook his head, and the anger and fight left his face. The sweet, overprotective, but seriously loving father was back.

He stood up, shook my hand, and thanked me. "If you weren't staying on top of all this, I would've probably done something stupid," he said. "Thanks for saving Crystal's career."

"That's my job." I smiled and walked him to the front lobby. "Oh, Mr. Rubin, don't tell Crystal what I said about the possible promotion. If she finds out, that could jeopardize it too. Joel has no tolerance for people who let ambition get ahead of their job." He nodded and left.

I went back to my office and sent an email to Joel. "Hey, just got a visit from my client's dad. Someone is trying to create some drama in your world. Just letting you know."

I was intentionally vague, but I only had one client in his show, and that was Crystal. Joel had accidentally let it slip that he was considering moving her up when he, Denim, and I were home watching the football game one night. Joel and Denim went to high school together, and had been tight friends ever since. They were president and vice-president of the LGBTQ support club for a while, but I could never remember which one held what position.

Mr. Rubin's visit was pretty-much how the rest of my day went. The boss was irritable, because of the morning gas leak, and true to form, he took it out on the rest of us. I had to deal with a minor crisis regarding one of my clients, who thought it would be a good idea to get stone-cold drunk at a bar the night before his show's opening. But, the final straw that made me want to crawl under my desk and cry, was when I found out that the client I had been courting for six months, took an offer with a different agency after having a torrid affair with the owner of said agency, that she'd met on a cruise. She didn't even have the decency to tell me. I found out when an email I had sent her confirming the date for signing documents was sent back *from our competitor*, telling me she had already signed with them.

I came home with a splitting headache, and utterly exhausted. I knew having the morning off seemed nice, but I prayed to the Gods, or whoever was listening, that I'd never have another half day thrust at me again. It just wasn't worth it.

I went into the kitchen, pulled out some Tylenol, downed enough to cut the pain, but not kill my liver, and then crashed on the couch. I didn't even realize I'd fallen asleep, until Denim came in with Clay in tow.

"You aren't ready?" Denim asked in frustration.

"Uuhhh, ready for what?" I asked.

"We're going out tonight to meet Suzie," he said with a duh expression on his face.

"Shit and fuck," I said. "I'm going to take a raincheck. Work was hell today."

"Oh no you're not," Denim exclaimed at the same time as Clay asked, "What?"

I looked at them both through slanted eyes, and asked, "What are you two playing at?"

Both of them looked sheepish, and I knew they were up to something.

"Listen," I said. "Suzie has no interest in me. I ran into her today, and she made it pretty clear I'm not her type." The expression on both of their faces confirmed that was what they were planning. "Not gonna happen, guys." I stood and started toward my room.

"Brother, please come. Do it for me. I want to spend time with you, and if you and Suzie aren't meant to be lovers, at least you can be friends."

I hesitated before going up the stairs to my bedroom. Sometimes, I really disliked my brother. He knew just the right buttons to push. The only saving grace was he seldom pushed them—only when he felt it was important.

I turned to him, eyes still slanted, and headache still there, but less intense, thanks to the meds. "Tell me why this is so important, and I'll consider it."

"Two reasons," he answered immediately. "One, Suzie saved our asses. I think Clay..." he looked at the guy and winked, "...and I would've let this go south if she hadn't been a hard ass. We owe her."

Clay returned Denim's look, and said, "And, she's also struggling with her brother leaving town. She was really depressed before I blubbered all over her. So, you see, she needs a distraction right now."

"And you want me to be her distraction?" I asked.

"I want us *all* to be her distraction," Clay responded.

I sighed, knowing I had already lost the battle. "Okay, what's the second reason?"

Both Clay and Denim made another distinctive expression that said they were up to something, then looked over at me. Denim finally said, "Because, you haven't been out on a date in almost a year. All you do is work, go to the gym, and sleep. I'm worried about you."

*Damn*, I thought. *He's still worried about my last shitty relationship. That was over a year ago. Why is he concerned about that now? I guess it's my fault.* After my ex, Sheila, dumped me for the producer, in order to further her career, I hadn't felt much like dating. For my brother's sake, maybe I needed to get back out there. If nothing else, then for appearances, and to get my brother off my back.

I'd also seen the sadness in Suzie's eyes myself, so to play the nice guy, I was willing to forget the whole,

"*You need a woman,*" comment from my gay brother, AKA 'old mother hen' who thought everyone had to be hooked up to be happy.

"One condition. We make it clear that I'm not there to flirt with her, or trick her into dating me. You two will have to split, and Denim, you'll sit next to me tonight, and Clay, you'll sit next to her, so there is no misconception about intentions. Deal?"

I could tell that condition was a tough one. Denim and Clay hadn't taken their hands off each other since they'd gotten back together. This was a good test, though. If they couldn't agree to that, then this was a setup, and they were still trying to play us.

Clay and Denim nodded at the same time.

"One of you will text her and let her know I'm coming, but that we've had this conversation, and she is not to feel uncomfortable about being set up."

Clay immediately protested. "If we do that, she won't come."

I shook my head. "That's a deal breaker for me. I'm not going to let you push me on a woman who doesn't want me—friend or not."

Clay sighed and looked at Denim. "I'll call her," he said.

Denim's face had gone all pinched and upset.

Why was this so damned important to him? I made a mental note to get to the bottom of it when it was just the two of us.

Clay went into the next room, and called Suzie. I could tell by the way he talked that she hadn't answered. "Suzie, it's Clay and Denim. I wanted to let you know we invited Denim's brother, Indi, to come with us. Hope that isn't a problem. See you in about an hour." Then, he hung up, and looked at me to see if that was adequate.

Although it wasn't exactly what I'd asked for, she had been warned I was coming, and that was about all I was going to get.

I went upstairs to grab a quick shower—my third one today. I would've skipped it, but work had been such a shithole mess, I knew I'd sweated up a stink. I looked at my bed, and wished I could just go crash there instead of going out, but Denim had pulled the *do it for me* card, so out I went.

I drove, and Denim sat in the front seat with me. We pulled up to Suzie's place right at 9 p.m., but she was nowhere in sight. Clay texted her to let her know we were outside, but got no response.

I couldn't stay in the street any longer, so I rode around the block, looking for a place to park. No surprise, there was nothing. Clay texted again to let her know we were riding around until she came out.

I made the loop at least fifteen times, and by nine thirty, there was still no response. "Guys, I think this is a bust," I said as we circled around again.

Clay tried to call her, but she didn't answer. He sighed, then agreed.

"Maybe she got scared off by the fact I'm coming," I said. Neither Denim nor Clay responded. "No big deal. Where do you want to go? The three of us can still go out."

They agreed, and we headed toward some dive called Vinnies' Diner that Clay and Denim said they frequented a lot. When we finished eating, we headed back to the townhouse, and I was lucky to find that elusive parking spot that was close enough to the town house and walk home.

Before I headed upstairs to crash, Denim apologized for Suzie standing us up. "I'm sorry we put pressure on you," he said.

"No problem, little brother, but you don't have to set me up. When I'm ready, I'm perfectly capable of setting myself up on a date."

He smiled, but it didn't hide the worry he banked behind his eyes.

# Suzie

Work was a disaster. My coworker who played Lydia, my lesbian lover in the show, had fallen during rehearsal and sprained her ankle. There were so many dance parts that were essential to the show that a bum ankle prevented her from performing. The shit crazy thing was, when they called her understudy, the woman had snuck off to London of all the damned places, and she couldn't make it back for rehearsal. They ended up pulling Alicia, my understudy, in for the part, but she had never done the routine. So, we ended up practicing until midnight. I came home to crash that night, then was up early the next day, and rehearsed all day for the performance that night. Luckily, Alicia was quick with the routine, so the show went off without a hitch.

I slept from the time I got home that night, until the next morning. The fifteen-hour sleep was what I needed to recharge. I jumped out of bed, and rushed to the theater to prepare for the next show. I didn't look at my phone until after I got home that night.

When I saw the texts from Clay, I almost crapped myself. I had forgotten all about our date. No problem. Clay would forgive me when he heard the shit-show I'd been dealing with. I almost texted, but saw I had messages, and figured Clay had called me too. If he was going to bitch me out, I should at least listen to his message before I called him.

When I heard Clay's message saying they had invited Indi, my heart did this weird, happy jolt thing, before I could suppress it with the anger of being set up on a date I didn't want. Despite what my treacherous libido was saying, the realization struck me that they must think I had stood them up, because the muscleman was going. God, would they think I was throwing away our friendships because of him? I immediately felt like the fuck of all fucks.

It was already 10 p.m., but Clay was a night owl like me, so I didn't hesitate to call. Unfortunately, Clay didn't pick up, so I left a quick message telling him that I'd been caught in a clusterfuck at work, and had just got done.

Then, I thought I'd better text him too, just in case. My text was basically the same. *"Just got done with show. Coworker fell. Been tit deep helping understudy learn part. You out?"*

I was just about to give up and go to bed, when I got a ding from the phone. *"You're a bitch, but still love you. Meet us at Vinnie's."*

I smiled. They were so forgiving. I wasn't sure about muscleman, though.

When I got to the diner, I saw Denim and Clay sitting in the far corner. I came up and sat across from them. They both stared at me without talking.

"Okay, you really *are* pissed," I said, throwing my stuff beside me.

Denim shook his head. "It was just a bad night to stand us up. But, it's our fault, not yours."

I could see there was turmoil in Denim's face, and Clay looked sad.

"What's going on? I didn't realize this was a big deal. I thought it was just a get-together."

Clay looked at Denim, and sighed. "See, this is where we fucked up. We were playing matchmaker with you and Denim's brother, Indi. When you didn't show, it blew up in our faces."

Denim shook his head, as he said, "We all screwed Indi, I'm afraid."

"I'm confused. What's the big deal? I'm sure your brother the muscle god isn't so hard up that getting stood up by me would send him over the edge." I chuckled at the thought. The man was so hot, I imagined women stood in line to fuck him.

Denim looked at me with an expression of both frustration and self-reprisal. "It really isn't my place to tell his business, but let's just say that about a year ago, he got screwed over really bad. He hasn't gone out with anyone since."

Clay jumped in, and added, "The man forced us to call you to let you know he was coming as a friend, so you wouldn't feel like he was forcing himself on you."

Denim then said, "So, when you didn't show, it basically was like he was being rejected again." He could see I was still confused, so he added, "I know my brother is the last person you'd think would be vulnerable with women, but the truth is, he has a very sensitive heart. He only dates when he finds someone he really likes. He never hooks up on one-night stands, and when he does find someone he likes enough to date, he gives his whole heart."

"I hate this, you guys, but I really was buried with work. I forgot about our date, and didn't know it was that big of a deal, or maybe I'd have been more attuned to it. I didn't even get home that night until late, and the next morning I was back at work early to prep my understudy for the part. I didn't see your messages until tonight."

Denim reached over and squeezed my hand. "This isn't your fault. It's mine. But I'm afraid I'm going to be in the doghouse for a while over this one."

"No doubt," I said, before I could stop myself.

He looked shocked, then laughed. "You are one of a kind, Suzie."

Then we were all back to normal, including my appetite. I ended my night on fatty carbs and milkshakes.

The next morning, I woke up early. It had been nagging me all night that this guy I thought was—or at least should be—a playboy was anything but. I kept trying to rationalize whether he was the sensitive guy his brother made him out to be. No matter how I mulled it over in my mind, I couldn't see him that way. He was just too damn gorgeous.

I got up and decided to go to the gym. The chances that he'd be there were slim. It was 8 a.m., and I guessed he was there long before that, at least by the look of those muscles. I would get a good workout in whether I ran into him or not, but if he was, maybe I could clear up why I'd stood him up.

I jogged down and came in warmed up. There was a new guy at the desk who had the look of a twelve-year-old. I'd swear the manager would be recruiting from elementary school next. He was nice enough and handed me my card back, and I went in to begin my stretches. I scanned the room, but Indi was nowhere to be seen. I was a little disappointed, but went on about my business. I was in my second repetition when a large shadow appeared above me.

My heart, the traitorous bitch, took a plunge into the abyss. Just like the first time I saw him, I lost my voice, and like my heart, my brain completely shut down. I made some kind of squeak, which made my face turn red.

My body went on autopilot, and lifted me up into a sitting position. The guy looked at me in a reserved and embarrassed way, and said, "I wanted to apologize for my brother and his boyfriend. I didn't know they hadn't told you I was coming, or I wouldn't have come out with them. I'm not the kind of guy that pushes myself on women." Then, he smiled, and said, "I'll leave you alone, but I just wanted you to know I'm not creeping on you."

As he turned to leave, I finally regained enough of my senses, to yell, "Stop!" a little bit too loud, which caused my face to get even redder than it was. "Your brother didn't tell you what happened?" I asked.

He shook his head. "I haven't seen him since yesterday morning."

I stood up, and allowed myself to stretch out the muscles I'd just worked, before he appeared over me. "I got caught up in a crisis at work. It was insane, and I didn't even look at my phone before last night. I didn't mean to stand you up, and I probably wouldn't have bailed on you if I'd had a normal night."

The guy didn't seem able to help himself, and asked, "Probably?"

I just shook my head. "I'm not one for being set up on blind dates. I can't promise I wouldn't have run the other way if I'd gotten the message. Truth is, I'd probably have called Clay back and told him to fuck himself." This admission caused both of us to laugh, and the ice between us broke apart just a little.

The guy was about to leave again, when something came out of my mouth that must have come from my traitorous heart. "Why don't we go grab a coffee when we're done here? I just have a few more reps."

He stared at me a moment too long, like he was warring with himself, whether he should take me up on the invitation. Of course, this stung my ego, and I was just about to call it off, when he responded, "Sure," he said hesitantly, then stuttered out another, "Sure, but only as friends, or friends of my brother's... ah... friend."

I could see his face turning red, and the vulnerable guy his brother said he was showed up, albeit just briefly.

I tilted my head. The feeling that I was the one pursuing and not the pursued, felt nice. Again, I began talking before I could stop myself. "So, this is a 'no-go' if I want to jump your bones?"

The guys face went from red to crimson, and he didn't seem to be able to find the words to respond, when I belted out a laugh that even I could hear echoed off the walls. "Get a grip, sport," I said. "I'm pulling your chain. Of course, as friends is the best." In my mind, I said, *Only way to make this work.*

He smiled, his face still red from embarrassment. "I'll go get my shower and change, then we can decide where to go. Does that work?"

I smiled back at him, amazed that I was enjoying our conversation as much as I was. Usually, when I was talking to a straight guy, especially one as hot as this one, I would be stuttering, and trying to figure out how to run away. There was just something different about this guy. Of course, my first thought then was, *He must be a closet case.*

# Indi

The woman was an enigma. She clearly had walls a mile high, but something, maybe because she felt bad about standing us up, had caused a mischievousness to come over her. My mind couldn't help wondering what it would be like to play around with that mischievous nature. I bet she was quite a piece of work in bed.

My own thoughts took me off guard. I had just put up a pretty significant boundary that this was strictly friendship, and already I was thinking about getting her into bed. I thought to myself, *Not cool, Indi, so not cool.*

I got my shower, forcing my mind not to think about her perfectly trim, muscular build, then got dressed. Unfortunately, I didn't have much time for hanging out. I had to be at the office  for a morning meeting. I texted my assistant to let her know I'd be there a little late, and to have all the paperwork ready for me, so I could just go right into the meeting without delay.

Suzie was waiting for me at the gym entrance, reading a magazine of some sort. She had slipped into a bright pink sweatsuit. I usually thought of pink sweatsuits as a Golden Girls flashback, but God help me, I would never think of it like that again, after seeing Suzie wearing one.

She smiled as I walked up to her. "I hope you don't mind going out with me wearing this. I jogged down today, and didn't bring a change of clothes."

I shrugged. "No problem with me," I said, but my stupid brain couldn't help thinking about what it would be like to taste her salty skin. She looked down, and I shook my head to get those thoughts out of my mind. I was quickly realizing I was never going to be able to be Suzie's friend. I was too attracted to her. Maybe I should admit that, and let her run away, like I knew she would.

She stood up, and we walked out of the gym. "There's a coffee shop just around the corner. Is that okay?" I nodded and followed her to the shop, deciding not to tell her I'd seen her there before, after she'd ducked out of the gym to avoid me.

Suzie was a riot once the façade of worry that seemed to surround her disappeared. Her natural gregarious personality seemed to take over. She had me laughing as she talked about her coworkers, crazy shit the audience had done during the show, and how they had to integrate it into the show, no matter how insane it was. At some point, there were several people involved in our conversation. It went from being just between us, to three or four people laughing at her antics. People were drawn to her, and why not? She was gorgeous, as well as funny and carefree. That kind of personality was infectious, and people seemed to get caught up in her web.

By the time I had to leave, we had both become comfortable in each other's company. I made my excuses that I had to run, and she stood up to go with me. The conversation had clearly evolved to include more than the two of us, so I told her, "You don't have to go on my account."

She appeared confused, and glanced around at the people we had been talking to, who were currently talking with one another.

As understanding came across her face, she said, "No, I need to go too. I'll walk you to your car." I nodded, and she said goodbye to the group.

"You have a real way with people," I said, when we were outside the shop.

"I like people." She grinned, and I knew she was telling the truth.

"It's fun to hang around you," I said. "I'd like to do it again." *Shit*, I thought. Hadn't I just told myself that I couldn't be friends with this woman? I had fought off one thought after another about kissing that beautiful mouth, or... well, let's just say *doing more.*

She nodded. "I'd like that too. In fact, the theatre's dark today, so what're your plans tonight? If you're free, you, Denim, Clay, and I can do a make-up date for the one I skipped out on."

Perfect, yes. And my brother would help keep my mind off the things I was imagining. "Yes, that sounds perfect," I said. "I'll text Denim and have them set it up."

She smiled at me, which sent electric shocks all over my body. Luckily, I made it to my car and left before I needed a cold shower to get through the rest of the day. As I drove toward my office through the ridiculous traffic that was New York, I chastised myself for acting like a nineteen-year-old man-whore, who couldn't keep his mind off sex. Suzie was an amazing, talented, and funny woman. Why couldn't I just enjoy being around her without making it about sex?

# Suzie

So, this was a huge mistake. I knew it, but like a moth to the flame, I couldn't seem to keep myself from making it. I was completely and utterly attracted to Indi. And what was with that name? Indi like Indiana Jones? His parents were not going to win any awards from their choices of names.

The crowd around us grew as I talked about attending the Conservatory in Kansas City, going from a karaoke queen to performing, and eventually losing *American Talent*, then, on to my being recruited to be on Broadway.

The entire time I droned on about myself, Indi sat back and watched. Occasionally he'd ask questions, but mostly, he just watched the show.

I knew I tended to put on a performance in front of people. I just accepted that was part of me. If there was an audience, I would perform. What shocked me was how well Indi handled it. I noticed he was amused by my silly antics. This, of course, just caused me to get worse, and before long, a group of people had joined us. We were all laughing, including Indi.

Usually, when I was attracted to a guy, my mind would shut down when I was with him, but I had to admit there was something different about this one. He was fun to be around. He didn't mind that hanging out with him wasn't just about him. Usually, when I ended up pulling in a crowd of strangers, the guy I was with would get antsy, like he owned me. Not that I'd been out with a ton of guys, but I'd been thrust into enough blind dates to get a good feel for the way most guys—or at least the ones I'd been set up with— operated.

# Indi

I puttered around nervously all day. Denim texted me back immediately after I asked if he and Clay were available to meet Suzie. I'd be damned if the man wasn't still trying to set me up with her. I couldn't seem to focus, knowing I was going to be in Suzie's presence that night. At one point, I was so ready to crawl out of my skin that I decided to sit down, and force myself to write down all the qualities in the woman that had nothing to do with her raw sex appeal.

It wasn't a hard list to write. The woman was oozing with talent. Not only was her body beautiful, and perfectly trimmed by her weightlifting, but she was also smart and sassy, which made her sparkle. I knew I would be able to spend countless hours with her just chatting. Of course, I also knew, if this morning was any indication, that being with Suzie also meant being around others, as she clearly loved people, and wanted as many of them involved in her conversations as possible.

It was hard to imagine someone who had become as successful as she had, being so comfortable with the public. Most of the actors and actresses I'd come across got the most minor level of fame, and it went straight to their heads. They would sometimes become paranoid that people were following them, or get some notion that they were no longer safe. That wasn't the case with Suzie. Of course, she hadn't quite hit the level of fame for the paparazzi to hound her. I was sure that would put a damper on things quickly, as those monsters seldom cared about the celebrity they were trying to get a photo of. The more hateful and hurtful the image, the more they tried to get it. Secretly, I hoped that would never be the case for the vivacious woman. Even though I'd only seen her work a crowd once, I loved watching her do it. Well, twice if you counted the time I went with Denim to see *Gerls*.

Now, all I had to do tonight was remember my list of all the amazing aspects of the woman that had nothing to do with my sexual attraction, and I'd surely be able to survive. Right? God, I hoped so, or I'd end up embarrassed before the evening was over.

I had plenty of time to change out of my work clothes and dress in something more appropriate for a night on the town. Clay and Denim had warned me that we would likely end up at a gay club at some point, so I wore the only outfit I had put aside for when Denim pulled me to one of those.

Early on, I figured out if I wanted to be a part of Denim's life, I had to be okay with his lifestyle, and for us that meant occasionally going out with him to gay dance clubs. One thing I learned quickly was that gay men could be handsy out on the dance floor. So, if I decided to dance in a gay bar, that meant I'd have to deal with possibly being felt up. I wasn't sure if all gay clubs were like that, but the ones that Denim had taken me to seemed to have a lot of handsy men in them.

The good thing was, there were usually a lot of straight women there too. Many went to avoid straight men, but that didn't mean they weren't willing to flirt with a straight guy if he showed up. In fact, that was where I'd met my last relationship–Sheila. Sheila was best described as a five-foot three female drag queen. She had spotted me across the crowded dance floor, and walked right up to me before she laid a hot, sexy kiss on me. How she knew I was straight, I never figured out.

Thinking about how that ended, though, I was pretty sure it would not be a good idea to try to find any of my future dates there.

We pulled up in front of Suzie's place, and I was immediately hit with *déjà vu*. Unlike last time, however, Suzie was standing on her stoop, ready to be picked up. I was glad I was driving and she was climbing into the back, because she had on black leather pants that were so tight, you could see all her incredible leg muscles through them. Her top was also black, with some kind of lacy pattern over it, and was cut deep in the front to show off her cleavage. I was literally afraid the drool would fall from my mouth just seeing her. God, help me, I wasn't going to survive the night, no matter how much I tried to focus on my list.

Suzie jumped in the back seat next to Clay and was all excitement. You could feel the energy level in the car change with Suzie's presence, and that was something else I liked about this woman. I guessed it wouldn't matter what kind of mood I was in, being around her would change it for the good.

The boys and Suzie had apparently decided we were going to their diner, and Suzie typed the address into her phone, and handed it to me for directions. "No need," I told her. "These two have already dragged me there before." I kept it to myself how I was unsure why anyone would want to go there.

To say it was a dive was being generous. However, when we walked in, everyone there seemed to know both Clay and Suzie. Within seconds after sitting, Suzie had a Coke in front of her and Clay had a small Diet Coke in front of him. Neither of them had ordered it, but neither seemed surprised that they arrived the way they did. The flirty waitress who brought them over, winked at me, stereotypically chewing gum with her mouth open, and asked what Denim and I would have.

The food at Vinnie's Diner was ho-hum, but being with Suzie was nothing if not exciting. As promised, Denim sat next to me and Clay across from him next to Suzie. It was obvious that she noticed this, and when we first sat down, she had a confused expression on her face. When she glanced over at me, however, I noticed when she figured it out. She smiled a bit, and I could tell she appreciated the effort.

It felt to me like we covered every subject known to man in the short time we sat together. I spent a good portion of the night confused as hell as to what the three of them were talking about. When I became so lost I had to ask questions, it was always about some obscure gay thing, and my questions just led to a lot of laughter—especially from my traitorous brother. When I gave him the "I can't believe you are letting me hang myself" glare, it would throw him and the other two into harder fits of laughter. So, finally, I decided to just sit back, grasp what I could, and enjoy the scenery in front of me. Of course, I mostly felt like a stalker, because watching Suzie was like watching a beautifully choreographed dance.

Her movements were fluid, and she had a way of gesturing with her hands, touching her face, and even putting her hand over her chest, that always sent me into a sexual haze. I know I recited the list of all her nonsexual, yet remarkable, qualities to myself at least a hundred times while we sat there.

If I thought the attention I gave her was masked, the quick glances she sent showed me I wasn't as good at hiding my feelings as I'd hoped. So, I worked harder at keeping my attention on Clay, or letting my eyes wander to other people in the restaurant, rather than gazing at her. I just hoped I wasn't creeping her out too much. Unfortunately, my infatuation prevented me from doing much to stop myself. I was falling hook, line, and sinker for this woman. Oh, well. At least I didn't have to worry about her ever wanting to see me again, so I would be able to keep myself under control after tonight.

After we ate, and as expected, I was dragged to the gay dance club down the street from the restaurant. Walking in, the place immediately erupted into a chant of, "*Beta! Beta! Beta!*" It took a moment for me to realize they were chanting for Suzie and Beta was her *very sexy* character in *Gerls*.

Suzie disappeared immediately into the crowd. I looked at Clay, and he just shrugged. "This is what she does," he said. "Might as well go get a drink. Denim and I are going to join her on the dance floor."

I went to the bar, and sat on an empty stool over to the right side of it. It was away from the main crowd, so I had a good vantage point, without attracting unwanted attention from the club's other occupants. The bartender brought me a Bud Light, and I turned the stool, so I could lean back and watch everyone dancing. More than once, a guy tried to catch my eye, but another lesson from hanging with Denim was *never* make eye contact, unless you wanted a man on you. I made the mistake only once, and after I had one guy sit in my lap, and another try to give me a blow job in the bathroom, I learned to focus on anything other than another guy's face.

I finally caught sight of Suzie as she was grinding a couple half-naked guys on the dance floor. My immediate reaction was rage. I shook this off, surprised that I felt this kind of jealousy for a woman I had just met, and certainly didn't have any claims to be jealous over. Not to mention, the guys grinding on her were obviously gay.

After the second or third dance, she eyed me sitting on the stool. An odd expression came over her face, and my first thought was that she had caught me staring, and was creeped out once again. I quickly looked away and ordered my second beer.

Before I could turn back around, she was standing behind me, her hand on my shoulder.

"Would you like to dance, Big Guy?" she almost whispered in my ear.

I knew for a fact that I shuddered before I could stop myself. I knew she was only speaking so close to my ear, because the music was too loud, but regardless, my body had reacted involuntarily to her presence, and that amazing voice. I was embarrassed to say, I was in no shape to stand for a moment.

I politely declined, and said I'd join her after I finished my beer. God knew I was going to need more than these two drinks, if I were going to make it through the night.

Unfortunately for me, Suzie, Denim, and Clay had also decided they needed to get drunk, so after I finished that second beer, I had to stop, realizing I was going to have to be the designated driver. God, I hated being the responsible one.

# Suzie

Seeing Indi sitting on the same bar stool where my brother Aiden always sat threw me. Aiden had been my foundation, and I could always depend on him, when I knew there was no one else to turn to. This rock of a man locked eyes on me while dancing, and the mixture of loneliness for Aiden and my sexual attraction to him, caused me to shudder a bit under his gaze.

I walked over, more out of habit than anything else, always picking Aiden up after the second dance with the boys, to drag him onto the dance floor. I didn't mean to startle him, but when I asked him to dance, a shudder went through him, which caused a similar reaction in me. I could almost imagine the naughty things I could do with him, to get a similar reaction out of him.

*Damn, where the hell have these thoughts come from?* I never allowed myself to fantasize about straight men that way. Actors, gay guys, anyone who was safe enough that I'd never have to worry about acting out those fantasies. Those were the people I thought about that way, not straight guys that might potentially be a threat. Something about this man sent my libido into overdrive. It was at this point I decided to marinate these thoughts in copious amounts of alcohol. If you couldn't conquer them, drown them—that was my philosophy.

I knew it was stupid, but I was totally inexperienced in these things. I truly didn't think about the fact that being with a guy I was attracted to and drinking alcohol would be a bad mixture. Unfortunately, this was a lesson I learned the hard way.

With the help of Denim, we were able to drag Indi onto the dance floor, but we all three instinctively knew we needed to keep as many men from pawing him as possible. If he were a closet case, or bi, I doubted he'd have minded, but the dance floor at this particular place was nothing if not handsy.

As the night went on, the boys and I became drunker and drunker, and finally, just before midnight, Indi began to wave us toward the door. "If the three of you drink any more, I'm not going to be able to get you to the car."

Of course, the three of us thought that was hilarious, and turned toward the bar for another round. Indi grabbed us all by the pants—at this point, I only had a tank top on, and Denim and Clay were shirtless, so pants were really his only option to grab. He pulled us out of the bar as we all protested loudly. He just laughed at us and shooed us down the road.

I had fallen asleep in the back seat before we reached my place, and the guys told me no one could rouse me, so they decided to go back to their place for the evening. I remembered arriving, and briefly waking up in the arms of the hunk whose name I couldn't quite remember. He carried me into the house, and deposited me onto their couch.

I woke up some time after everyone had gone to bed, and it took me a moment to remember I was in the hunk's home. Damn, I had to pee. I wandered around the house for what felt like an hour, before I finally found a bathroom. When I came out, I decided I wanted to see the hunk again, but accidentally walked in on Denim and Clay, buck naked in an awkward position. They both yelled at me, and I giggled as I backed out of their room. I wandered on further down the hall and opened bedroom doors, until I found the hunk lying on his back, shirtless, and in some skimpy shorts.

I remembered going into the room, crawling on top of him and laying a kiss on his gorgeous mouth. He must have been asleep, because he jumped up, almost knocking me onto the floor. I began stripping off my shirt and telling him something about having his children. I honestly didn't remember much more than that.

The next morning, I woke up half-naked in a bed I didn't recognize. *Oh shit! What have I done?* was the first thought in my head. The second thought was, *Oh shit! My head!* I looked around the room, trying to find any evidence that I had slept with someone, but at this point, my head was pounding so hard, I couldn't seem to stream together any thoughts to figure out who. I slowly got out of bed, trying to keep the pounding to a minimum, and went into the ensuite, trying to find the guy I'd apparently slept with.

I didn't find the guy, but I did find a toilet, which I desperately needed, and a sink to wash my face in. I wandered out of the bedroom, and froze immediately, remembering walking in on Clay and Denim. Fuck! That memory was immediately followed by my basically seducing Indi. *Fuck!! I don't even remember stripping off my top!*

I became angrier at that moment. I was sure the muscleman had taken advantage of me while I was drunk. I guessed, in that moment, the thought that he was a gentleman was outside of my ability to reason. I could blame it on the hangover, but the reality was, the fucking idiot Eddie from high school was still all in my head.

The message that seemed to reside in my muscle memory was all straight men were evil, raping bastards who couldn't be trusted. The anger became steaming hot. Apparently, hot enough to overcome the hangover, and I stomped through the house to find the asshole, before I blew a gasket.

I found my prey in the living room, with his large frame hanging over the sofa, drool dripping from his half-opened mouth. If I had any conscious thought that existed outside of the hangover and the anger, I would have noticed he had not slept in the bed, but rather had slept on the couch. But conscious, coherent thought was still far from my hungover ability.

Upon seeing him laid out on the couch, I immediately began yelling at him. "You son of a bitch, you'd take advantage of a woman when she was half drunk, and not able to make a reasonable choice?"

Clay and Denim rushed down the stairs hearing my tirade.

Indi woke up with a start, wiping a hand down his face as he tried to figure out what the crazy screaming woman was saying. Finally, he found his voice and asked, "What the fuck are you talking about?"

Still unable to be rational, I screamed, "I woke up half-naked in your bed. Explain that!"

Denim and Clay were shooting daggers at him, and it was evident that Indi was still trying to figure out what was going on.

Denim walked over and stood between me and his brother, his eyes murderous as he stepped toward him. "Did you have sex with her last night?" he asked.

"I most certainly did not, even though she came into my room when I was already asleep, climbed on top of me, began stripping, and told me we were going to have three children."

My face turned red, because I did remember doing just that.

"Then what the fuck is she going on about?" Denim asked incredulously.

"I have no *fucking* idea," he moaned, just waking up and gathering his wits. "As I said, she came into my room and climbed on top of me, waking me up. I jumped out of bed, and she rolled over and took off her top. Then, I immediately left, came down here, and went to sleep on the couch. I sure as hell never touched her."

I immediately knew he was telling the truth. I had tried to seduce him, although at the moment, I couldn't tell you why, except that he looked like some kind of god lying in that bed without a shirt on.

I nodded, and said, "Yeah, I think he is telling the truth." Then, without the anger, my headache returned with a vengeance. "Oh fuck!" I said, and fell back into a chair. If my head didn't feel like it was going to roll off my body, I thought the mortification would have driven me from the house, but as it was, I could barely move, much less run.

"God, Indi, I'm so sorry. I just had a bad experience once, and I have trust issues." I tried to explain more, but then my stomach decided it would like to cleanse itself of all the contents from the night before. I had no idea where anything was in the house except for the front door, and so I dashed for it, threw it open and puked off the side of the stoop.

"God, could this get any more embarrassing?" I said aloud to myself, after emptying my stomach.

Denim came over and wrapped his arm around me, pulling me back into the house and into the kitchen. "We all need to deal with our hangovers. Then, we can deal with the rest."

Denim, Clay, and I sat at the kitchen bar, all three of us with our heads in our hands. Indi was whipping something up in the blender, which we all felt more than heard. He placed a glass of something foul in front of each of us, and demanded we drink them. "Hangover remedy," he said, a wicked smirk forming on his face.

We all tried to drink the foul liquid only to gag. "Drink it," he demanded. "You'll feel better. I promise."

"He's right," Denim agreed. "It's disgusting, but it works." Denim downed his, and I'd swear his face turned as green as the liquid he had just drank. Clay followed, and the entire room turned to me.

"No, nope, I've already puked. I don't want a repeat."

"Drink it," Indi demanded, and for some reason, I did. Oh, it was so nasty. Something along the lines of, if seaweed had a baby with kale. I gagged, but nothing came up, so I put my head down and willed the horrible headache, the embarrassment, and the nasty liquid I'd just drunk to go away.

Within a few minutes, the headache began to recede. "What was in that?" I asked, amazed that I would have my head back this early after treating it.

Indi just smiled, and said, "An old family recipe."

Within thirty minutes, the headache was banked, and I felt like a human again. I turned to my other two hangover buddies, and obviously, they had begun to feel the same.

"Drink at least two full glasses of water before you get up," Indi demanded of us. "That should pretty much fix it." He slid a glass of water in front of each of us.

I looked up at the man in front of me, and frowned. "I'm sorry I accused you," I said, the embarrassment overtaking me again.

"No need. I can see how you drew that conclusion. You were very drunk last night." He didn't chuckle, nor did he make eye contact. I could tell he was still upset by the accusation. Hell, I would be too. I knew I had to explain why I had reacted this way if I were going to ever be able to face him or Denim again.

"When I was a teenager..." I paused for a moment, knowing I'd not be able to tell the whole story, so I went with what I could. "When I was a teenager," I began again, "I had something happen, and ever since then I have had PTSD around men. When I woke up with the hangover, I jumped to the conclusion that you had followed through with what I'd started. If I'd had the ability to string two thoughts together, I probably wouldn't have jumped to that conclusion. So, I'm really sorry."

The man just stared at me with those beautiful eyes of his, and said, "I've never taken advantage of a woman—or a man..." as he looked over at his brother and his boyfriend, "...and I never will. You are and always will be safe with me. That is a promise I can make without hesitation."

I nodded, relieved he didn't hate me, and my heart leaped a bit at the serious statement he had made about being safe with him. I almost couldn't reconcile in my head how a straight guy could be someone I'd feel safe with... and, damn, even I knew how fucked up that sounded.

This man confused the hell out of me, but despite basically accusing him of taking advantage of me, which he clearly was innocent of, his expression held compassion mixed with sexual desire. For at least the dozenth time since meeting this guy, I asked myself what I'd gotten myself into.

# Indi

I had been sound asleep when the woman came down the stairs in a screaming huff. The anger in her eyes was wild, and frankly, she scared the shit out of me. Amazingly enough, I wasn't angry about the accusation. Rather, I was upset for her. What could have happened to someone that would cause them to jump to that conclusion without knowing the facts? I was proud of my brother's reaction. He stepped in between Suzie and me, and the look that he burned me with showed a man who would go to any lengths to defend those who'd been taken advantage of. All this, of course, warred with my own feeling of innocence.

When I pointedly told them all that as soon as Suzie began stripping, I left and came downstairs to sleep, the anger immediately disappeared, and was replaced by embarrassment. Luckily, she recognized the truth. Had she been any drunker, I was not sure she would have remembered. *Note to self, the next time a beautiful young woman comes to my home drunk, lock your bedroom door!*

I was waiting for Suzie to run, but apparently her hangover kicked back in after the anger faded, and she turned green in front of me, even puking out the front door. I went into the kitchen and made my special hangover smoothie. I usually had it made beforehand, but didn't know I'd need it today, and I put it in front of each of them. After much prompting, they each drank their glasses, and as I knew it would, the concoction worked. I could see their expressions clearing as their hangover headaches began to dissipate.

As I watched them, Suzie kept looking back at me. I could see she regretted her reaction, and she seemed to have something she wanted to say. I'd seen abuse victims before. I knew she was warring with herself about what or how much to say, so I didn't press.

Finally, when her headache had subsided enough, she faced me and said something happened when she was a teen. Then, she apologized again.

I wanted to gather her up in my arms. She appeared to be so lost and vulnerable. This wasn't the powerful Suzie Fisher I was used to seeing. I knew touching her would just send her back into the traumatic past, so instead, I did the only thing I could do. I locked eyes with her, and told her the truth about me. "I've never taken advantage of a woman… or a man…" Then, I looked pointedly at my brother and his boyfriend, and continued, "…and I never will. You are, and always will be, safe with me. That is a promise I can make without hesitation."

The look on Suzie's face changed. It was slight, but I could see something fall away that was immediately replaced with the same curious look she always seemed to have when she considered me. For someone who had been hurt in the past, I was sure there was always a part of them that was watching out for the bad guy. I could only imagine how exhausting that must be. I knew my words would never be enough, but my actions could. If Suzie gave me the chance to get to know her, she would learn that she was safe and secure with me. If she didn't give me the chance, hopefully, she'd remember at least one straight man was safe to be around. Either way, I'd be happy.

I thought as I gazed at her, *It isn't like I don't want her.* I didn't think I'd ever felt this kind of longing, at least not since I was a teenager. Back then, it was more of a longing for the girls I knew I'd never have a chance with. The memory of that sexy, perfect body molding into mine as she attempted to seduce me was etched into my memory. I knew that had left some permanent scars on me. It would be a long time before I could look at another woman and not see her.

I left the group, and went upstairs to get ready— this time making sure my bedroom door was locked. I let the shower run a little colder than I normally would, with hopes that my mind wouldn't get caught up on those perfect breasts. I couldn't even touch myself to the fantasy of her, knowing how she felt about what had happened, but that wasn't something I'd be able to do forever. *May the female gods forgive me,* but she stirred every sexual impulse inside me.

My workday went fine, and because I missed my morning workout, I went after work. I didn't feel much like being social, so after I got home, I went to my room—again locking my door—and relaxed with a book in bed. This was pretty much my routine until the weekend.

***

As I suspected, I couldn't get Suzie out of my head. I knew I would call her if I didn't keep myself occupied, and I was not going to do that. If the woman wanted to see me, she would have to make the first move. The only thing I could do was find a place as far away as possible to prevent this.

I thought about going to the Hamptons, and staying at my parents' beach house, but the place would be boring by myself. My mom had been trying to get Denim and me to fly out to Denver, and it was early enough in spring that there was probably still good skiing on the mountain, but the last thing I wanted was Mom prying into my personal business, and beginning the whole grandkid thing. For the life of me, I would never understand why someone who was so bad at raising her own children, would ever want to have grandkids.

I finally decided on a drive to New Haven, to visit my best friend, Dalton, who had settled there after we graduated from college. Sure enough, he was free for the weekend, and said I could stay with them.

Dalton had married Kristina, his sweetheart from the University, who met me at the door, and pulled me into a big hug. I knew the minute the woman wrapped her arms around me, I had made the right choice to come here. "Dalton had to run a couple of errands for me," she explained. "But, that's good, 'cause once he gets here, I won't be able to get a word in edgewise. What's been going on with you?"

I laughed, knowing she was right. Once Dalton and I were reconnected, we tended to talk about everything under the sun. Except for my brother, Dalton was the only other person I could confide in about everything in life.

"I'm good," I assured Kristina. "Maybe a little bit in a rut, but that's to be expected, I guess."

She shrugged. "Only if you let it be. How's your love life?"

I knew this was coming, since Kristina asked this every time I saw her, or spoke to her on the phone.

"It's about the same as last time we spoke," I told her.

"Then it's shit," she said.

I couldn't help, but laugh. Kristina wasn't one to mince words, and she had been trying to get me married off since long before she and Dalton had tied the knot.

"It's exactly how I want it," I told her. "Unlike Dalton, not everyone has to be married to be happy."

She thought about what I said, trying to figure out if there was an insult in it, but after a second of thought, she just shrugged. "You're the marrying type, too, my friend, but you already know this, don't you?"

I didn't want to argue, especially since she was probably right. I preferred to be with other people. I wasn't a loner, and the past few weeks, while Denim and Clay got closer and closer, I had felt more and more alone. Despite that, however, I knew bad relationships were worse than being lonely, so I was in no hurry to get hitched, just for the sake of it.

I changed the subject, and asked Kristina what they had been up to, and her cheeks turned pink. I smiled at the change, and knew something big must have happened.

"Okay, spill," I said.

"Not until Dalton gets home, then we have some news."

I looked at her, and immediately knew what the news was, but I would never spoil the surprise. "Okay, have it your way. Tell me about work."

We chatted for about an hour before Dalton got back. When he walked in and saw me, he pulled me into a big bear hug. "Damn, Indi, I've missed the shit out of you!"

"Same here," I replied. "How've you been?"

"About as good as a man can be," he said, then winked at his wife.

Dalton and Kristina had always been affectionate, but this was out of character. Anticipating the news, I prompted, "Okay, both of you, out with it. What's going on?"

Kristina sighed. "Okay, okay. If you must know, we've joined a cult, and I'm marrying a second husband."

Dalton almost choked. "And what the hell cult is that?" he asked.

"Honey, you are the worst at following through with a joke," she huffed. "We're pregnant," she said, and then she screamed and jumped in my arms.

I glanced over at Dalton, and the expression on his face as he stared at his wife could only be described as a mixture of shock and pure love. When he noticed me looking at him, he smiled wider, and said, "Can you believe it? I'm going to be a dad."

"Yes, I can believe it, and you'll be a great dad, and…" I picked Kristina up and hugged her again. "…you are going to be the best mom! This calls for a celebration. Carry out or dine in?"

"PIZZA!" both Kristina and Dalton cried out at once.

We all went down to the pizza place we ate at every time I came to town to see them. This was our tradition since we were in college together. At one point in our friendship, I thought I might get so sick of pizza that I'd never eat it again. But, despite the fact we pretty-much lived on it for four years, I never did, and if I got together with these two friends, it was inevitable that we'd order it at least once, but more likely several times during our visit together.

As we ate, Kristina talked non-stop about the pregnancy. She had just moved into her second trimester, and so they had decided to start telling family and friends. Kristina's mom had struggled with miscarrying, Kristina being the only infant to make it full-term, so they had been extremely cautious, so as not to bring heartache back to her mom.

"So far, the pregnancy is going well," she assured us, but I could tell she was trying to convince herself.

"So, am I going to be *Uncle Indi* then?" I asked.

Kristina and Dalton looked at each other, then back to me. "Maybe a little more," Dalton said.

I cocked my eyebrow, not knowing exactly what he was going to say, but decided to rib him a bit. "No, I will *not*, under any circumstances, become your brother husband."

Kristina burst into laughter, and Dalton just stared a hole through me. He looked at his wife, and said, "Now see what you've started? This is going to be a thing for the rest of our lives."

I chuckled, before Kristina put her hand over mine. "Dalton and I want you to become the baby's godfather."

I stared at them both, genuinely surprised. "Have you two lost all access to your senses?" I asked. "How the hell would I be able to manage a feat such as that?"

"Because, you have a heart of gold, and if anything ever happened to us, you would know us better than almost any other people on the planet," Kristina replied.

"And, you hold your liquor better than anyone I know, and since the godfather tends to be the one to take the kid out on their twenty-first birthday, you can drink him or her under the table, and still be able to get them home safely."

I just shook my head, "Glad you are thinking ahead, Dalt."

"So, will you consider it and let us know?" Kristina asked.

"I don't need to consider anything," I replied. "If the two of you are insane enough to turn me into your offspring's godfather, who am I to say no?"

Kristina jumped up out of the chair, upending it as she moved, and landed in my arms. "I can't tell you how excited we are!" she yelled, and then the waterworks started. "Damn these hormones," she said. "Any emotion and I'm crying."

"Or, biting my head off," Dalton said between his teeth.

Kristina pinned him with a glare. "Keep that up, and you'll see just how uncomfortable you can get."

Dalton smiled, got up from his seat, and took his wife from me, lifting her into his arms. "My Beautiful, I'm just thankful you are willing and able to do all the demanding work of bringing our little one to life. If you're a bit irritable, that's a small price to pay."

She continued to eye him with suspicion. "You're good with your words, literary man, but I'm on to you," she said as she pulled out of his arms.

"Okay, I'm going to go pee, and then you two can escort me home, where I'm going to sit in the tub for an hour or so. Indi, tomorrow, I'll go over some of the godfather stuff with you, but for now, you and my sweet-talking husband can catch up."

She leaned over and kissed me on the cheek, then flipped the bird to Dalton, which caused him to burst into laughter. "If you are up to it, Dear," he said with a wink.

"Not with Indi in the house," she said flippantly as she walked toward the bathroom.

When we got back to their house, Kristina kissed me on the cheek again, and told me how happy she was that I was there, and had agreed to be the godfather. Then, as promised, she disappeared up the stairs.

"You are going to be a fucking dad! What the fuck?" I said, when she was out of hearing range.

"I know," he said, his eyes taking on a mystified expression. "We weren't even trying. Kristina had a bad reaction to her birth control, and so we decided that if she went off, we could handle her getting pregnant. The doctor told her it was unlikely to happen any time soon, due to her hormones being wigged out, because of the meds, but a few months later, here we are."

"Are you ready for this?"

"Oh, hell no. Can you really be ready to be a dad?" He shook his head. "No, I think it just happens, then you do what you have to do to get ready."

"Well, I wasn't kidding," I told him. "You'll both be excellent parents, and I am going to be a *damned awesome* godfather. I am totally going to make that kid impossible to live with."

Dalton just shook his head. "I have no doubt of that, Indi! *No doubt!*"

The rest of the weekend was relaxing and fun. Kristina had books about godparents, and what it meant, and I indulged her by letting her fill me in on all my new responsibilities. At one point, Kristina's parents even came over and talked to me about my new role. This was quite a bit more formal than I expected, but I was excited about it too.

I made sure they knew that despite attending a religious private school, I wasn't particularly religious, but both Dalton and Kristina assured me this was more about making sure their kid had someone to support and love them as they grew up.

Secretly, I was bouncing up and down inside from the news. I knew I would always love my best friend's kid, but now I was actually, officially, going to be a part of its life. It felt wrong to call it an it. "Do you know the sex yet?" I asked.

"No," Dalton said. "We haven't found out yet. They said it's around four to five months before they can tell."

"Hey, we're going to have a gender reveal party. You wanna come to that? As soon as we know for sure, we're going to tell everyone."

"You bet your ass, I'll come," I said. "I need to know if I will be spoiling a boy or a girl rotten!"

He laughed. "God, this whole thing was probably a horrible idea. What were we thinking?"

I punched him in the arm as he laughed. "You were joking, but I do intend to be the crazy, fun godparent that fills the kid with candy just as I'm bringing them home from eating ice cream."

Dalton was the happiest I'd ever seen him, and I would think he would be. I couldn't even imagine what it would be like to find out you were going to be a parent. No, it was beyond my ability to reason that out. I barely kept my own life together—much less the life of someone else.

But the life of a godparent! *That*,  I *knew* I could do. My own godparents were from Ireland, so I didn't get to see them often. When they were around, it was like being surrounded by adults who were looking for ways to make us beyond spoiled. My parents were whack jobs, and I thought our godparents realized that, so when they were around, they tried to shower us with as much love as they could give. I had good examples to model my own godparent responsibilities after.

The night after Dalton and Kristina asked me, I texted my brother and my godparents, and let them know I was going to continue in their footsteps. I got texts back the next morning with a list of do's and don'ts. Mostly the do's revolved around never sparing a dime, providing copious amounts of chocolate candy, and never hesitating to play video games. The don'ts involved never letting parents know your devious plans of spoiling the child before they occurred. *Forgiveness rather than permission* was the general theme of the don'ts. I couldn't help taking my computer down and sharing the list with Dalton and Kristina, who laughed, but also looked concerned. That just made it all the more fun for me.

I got back to the city refreshed and happy. To my surprise, I spent the entire weekend not thinking about the beautiful woman who had come into my room and lain on top of me. But the moment I walked into my home, I was greeted by her intoxicating scent. All the memories came back to me like a tsunami. That wave was followed by another when the woman herself appeared from around the kitchen, wearing an apron. The sight of her wiped everything else from my mind, and I was struck dumb. I almost tossed my bag down and pulled her into my arms. You'd think she was my lover the way I wanted to respond. Luckily, I stopped myself before I did anything embarrassing.

# Suzie

I ndi seemed to be ignoring me, and I couldn't blame him for it. The more I thought about our mishap—no, not *our* mishap, *my* mishap—the more disgusted with myself I had become.

By Friday night, I was in a total funk. I went to the club to dance it all out, but couldn't seem to find my dance legs, so I went to Vinnie's instead. Clay found me there an hour later, pumped full of sugar, fat, and carbs. I had my head down on the table when he walked up.

When I told him I missed my baby brother, and couldn't seem to shake the sadness of that, he gathered me up in his arms and texted Denim to meet him there instead of the club. The two of them dragged me around with them, cheering me up and plying me with alcohol. At first, I refused to drink, remembering the horrible events our last evening out had come to, but Denim assured me Indi was out of town for the entire weekend, so I was in no danger of repeating my striptease.

I didn't embarrass easily, but that comment put my face in a full-out blush. Leave it to the evil bitches to bring that back up when I was down and out. Of course, I couldn't help laughing it off. Behind the hateful truth, were two people who were quickly becoming my besties—and with Aiden now in Eastern Washington, I needed besties really bad.

Sunday morning, we all slept in, and by noon, we were just beginning to nurse our hangovers. Clay had the idea that we should fix baked goods, and so we all donned aprons and went about the process. Apparently, none of us could cook worth shit, so it was more of a fun experience, than it was a process of fixing edible food.

By the time we made an attempt at cinnamon rolls, crescent rolls, and some Slovenian cake Clay had suggested, we had wasted the day away. Sunday was one of the rare days I didn't have a rehearsal, or a performance, and I had dreaded being home alone all day, so, I was more than happy for the diversion. What none of us had remembered was Indi would be coming home. I walked around the kitchen after cleaning up a thousand dishes, and was wiping down the counter, when I looked up to see Indi staring at me from the doorway.

The expression on his face could have melted wax. It wasn't an angry expression, it was worse—it was pure hunger. I lost my breath, and stood like an idiot staring at him, before Denim came around me, saw his brother and greeted him, which apparently was not something I had the skill to do myself.

When I was finally able to pull my eyes away from him, I turned back into the kitchen to catch my breath. Clay saw me and squinted his eyes, then pulled me into the laundry room, pointed his finger at me, and said, "Spill. What's up with you and Indi?"

I just shrugged. I didn't know what to tell him. Something about the man got in my head... and in other more discreet areas.

He stared at me for a moment longer, and then shook his head. "I'm going to tell you this. You and Indi have to work out this love/hate thing you've got going on, because it is radiating some seriously bad vibes into our little tribe. *Capisce?*" he said. I just nodded, not knowing what to say. This thing seemed outside of my control.

When we came back out, Indi had gone up to his room. I decided that was my cue to end the visit, and despite the visual daggers Clay sent me, I kissed them both, thanked them for saving me from a weekend of being sad, lonely Suzie, and headed out the door.

I didn't make it to the subway, before my phone pinged. It was Indi, "Where'd you go?"

"Sorry, I have to head home."

"No, you don't. You're avoiding me. Why?"

Well, that sucked. I wasn't usually that obvious, and when I was, people didn't usually call me on it.

"I'm sorry. It just felt awkward. Do you hate me?"

"Of course not. Let's go for a beer. I have good news."

I texted an excuse about needing to get to sleep, but erased it. Clay was right. We needed to figure this out, before it destroyed our friendship.

"Okay. Where?"

"Meet me at the door. There's a place about a block away."

I walked back to his door, and he was waiting for me outside. "Thanks," he said as I arrived.

"For what?" I asked.

"For being brave enough to come back."

I could see his expression was genuine. "Let's walk and talk," I said, and he came down the stairs.

As we strolled along the street, I figured I should just get things out in the open. I could almost hear Clay prompting me, which gave me courage.

"Indi, I like you, probably more than I should." God, my heart was beating so fast, I thought it might explode, and I wasn't being clichéd. I was feeling like I could hyperventilate at any moment.

"I... I'm..." I had to stop to catch my breath. Why was this so damned hard?

Indi came over and put his hand on my shoulder as I bent over. "Suzie, are you all right?"

"No. No, I don't think so," I managed to say.

"Look at me," Indi commanded. "You never have to be afraid of me. You can say whatever you need to."

His comments calmed me, at least, enough so I could breathe. We walked across the street to a bench next to a bus stop, and sat down.

"I'm not an easy-going woman." I sighed. "Dating a man scares the shit out of me." I chuckled a little at the understatement of the century. "I doubt you are really interested in all this baggage, and I kept thinking you must be gay, but…" I realized I was babbling, and the look on his face when I said he was probably gay, caused his left eyebrow to rise in a comical way.

I drew in a breath to apologize, when he moved within inches of my mouth. He hesitated, waiting for me, and I quickly closed the distance between us. *Oh my god! What an amazing kiss!* I could melt and turn to putty with that kiss.

When he pulled back, he looked me in the eye, and said, "My brother is the most important person in my life. I love him completely and utterly, and would go to the moon and back if he needed me to, I have no problem with him or anyone else being gay, but I can assure you one hundred percent that I am not! I have had more than a few opportunities, and more than a few men have felt me up, so I know without a shadow of a doubt, dick don't float my boat."

When he looked at me, my face flushed, but this time not in embarrassment, but sexual heat.

"I have not made the moves on you, because you made it clear you didn't want me to, and unlike the high-school guy you told us about, I will never move on a woman if she doesn't want me to."

I opened my mouth to say something, but I found, as was becoming a trend with this guy, I had nothing to say. So, instead, I reached up, pulled him down and kissed him with all the words that I couldn't form.

No man had ever been so patient with me. It was like he could see inside my head, and comfort the screaming fear monsters that lived there.

When I pulled away, his eyes were glazed over. "Suzie, I want you more than I can express."

We kissed, my willingness apparently all the permission he was looking for, and he deepened it. His tongue found mine, as our teeth clacked together. His hand came down over my back, and he pulled me gently toward him.

My libido kicked in, and my hands slipped under his shirt and began exploring his body. His explored mine and skidded up and down the outside of my blouse. I had never hated having my shirt tucked in more than I did right then. I wanted skin on skin. I wanted him to kiss me, while those big, hard, hands perused my body.

He stood up. "Suzie, if we stay here, I'm guessing we'll both have an indecent exposure on our record."

I laughed, and all but purred as I stood up, sliding into his arms. "Wouldn't it be worth it?" I teased.

A low growl emanated from deep inside him.

I trailed my hand across his rough chin and whispered in his ear, "Let's forget that beer and go back to your place?"

He pulled away from me, despite the sexual desire and raw lust in his eyes, and asked, "Are you sure, Suzie? I don't want to move too fast."

I sat back down. "You're right. This isn't me. It was too fast. Fuck!" I all but shouted with frustration, "...but I want this to be me!" Indi chuckled, pissing me off. "Hey, a little sympathy here."

Indi sat next to me, "You don't have to rush things with me. We can take things as slow as you need them. Come on, let's have that beer."

Being with Indi was easy. He was laid back, and excited that he'd been asked to be the godparent of his best friend's baby to be. It was sweet seeing that he wanted that responsibility. We chatted about his godparents, and how they spoiled him, and how he had plans to do the same with this one.

We strolled hand-in-hand on the way back to his place. I found I wanted him to touch me, to have his hands on me, and I was surprised this didn't scare me more than it did. I guessed it was all because he was so willing to be patient, and not push anything until I was ready. But, ready as I was, I wouldn't be able to jump him and pull him back to his place for a massive sexcapade. This slow and easy, I thought I could do.

Clay and Denim were nowhere to be seen when we came back to his house. I decided to make a move, and see what happened.

When we came inside, I pulled him down for a kiss. "I like you, Indi. Wanna take it to another level with me?"

My heart had begun beating wildly as I waited for his answer.

"Suzie, I won't say no, because I want you, but the ball has to be in your court. You take this as fast or as slow as you need to."

I laughed and punched him in the shoulder. "Okay, okay, you've made your point. You're a gentleman. Let's try," I said.

We sat on the couch. Or rather, Indi sat on the couch, and I sat on him. It was like some wanton woman had taken over my body. I would blame it on my character, Beta, but the truth was, this was all me.

We made out like we were still a couple of kids in the back seat of a car, and as Indi promised, I was one hundred percent in control.

Finally, again totally surprised at myself, I stood and pulled him up. "Wanna try out the bedroom?"

Indi looked sexed up and ready to go, but he hesitated. "Oh, you know *I* wanna take this to the bedroom, but do *you*?"

I nodded sheepishly. "But, you'll go slow?"

He nodded in response, and I pulled him up the stairs.

He lay on the bed as I took off my top and pants, leaving only my panties and bra on. It was like instincts had taken over. The fear was still there, but it was banked. I hesitated only momentarily, before crawling into bed next to him. He ran his finger along my side slowly, letting it circle the edges of my bra.

The sensation sent chills all over my body. I'd never let a man get this far. Just the reminder of that caused me to panic. I tried to lie still, but Indi was too perceptive. He sat up and put his back up against the headboard.

"You're supposed to tell me when something is happening."

I was fighting the tears that threatened to spill. "Am I ever going to be able to do this without freaking?" I asked out loud, knowing he wouldn't have the answer, but needing to ask anyway.

He answered, "Yeah, you will, but not if you don't listen to what you need. Suzie, I'm not sure why you pushed this tonight. I love it, don't get me wrong, but you need to get that I just wanna be with you. I liked having the beer with you tonight. I liked that you let me go on and on about becoming a godparent. I loved that you didn't tell me I was being a homespun idiot for being excited about it. It all just made me happy."

I didn't move, and instead stared up at the ceiling as he spoke. Of course, being so exposed caused me to be self-conscious, especially with him being so sweet about it all.

"Suzie, look at me, please."

I got up to grab my shirt and pulled it back on, then sat on the bed opposite him.

"We can go as fast or as slow as you need. That wasn't me just placating you, or saying something to get you to a point so I could move on you. It's simple. I wanna be your friend, and if it turns to something else, then great. I won't lie, I'd also like to be your lover, but seriously, give yourself a break, okay?"

I nodded, feeling totally self-conscious, and a whole lot like a stupid teenage girl who'd got too involved with an older guy. I hated that I felt like I was the same age as when the idiot tried raping me. I hated with my entire being, how that still affected me.

"Wanna share your thoughts?" Indi asked.

I sighed, "Not particularly, but yeah, it sucks that after all this time, that horrible boy still has this much power over me. I want to be like Clay and Denim, or my brother, or other gay guys, and just let myself be sexual, and not freak out about it."

Indi chuckled, "Well, you know, that's sort of a myth. I've been around a lot of gay guys, and not all of them are sluts. I mean, they are guys, and the stereotype about guys being sex pigs is usually true, but I've met a couple who are in the exact same place you are. They were hurt, and as a result, have to take things slow."

I knew he was right. I'd met gay men who struggled with intimacy, because of childhood abuse, but it was easier to see the gay community as a whole, as an open and sexually liberated group.

"I think I should go, Indi," I said, and started to get up.

Indi didn't try to stop me, but instead said, "You know, we can just cuddle."

I turned back around and looked at him. "Wouldn't that be weird?"

He chuckled. "Not to me. I'm happy to start there, and let the other stuff happen as it will."

I loved that idea, and now that I had my top back on, I felt a whole lot less vulnerable. "Yes," I said, "Let's try that."

I crawled back over to Indi, and kissed him as he wrapped his arms around me, so we spooned each other. "You okay?" he asked, after pulling the covers up over us.

"I'm okay," I replied honestly. "This feels good."

Indi's chuckle was low as he lifted the hair from my neck, and placed a gentle kiss there. "It really does," he agreed.

We both fell asleep like that, and I woke up later. I untangled myself and went to pee. When I came back, Indi was still lying in the position I'd left him. He was so beautiful. I knew a rugged bodybuilder wasn't supposed to be beautiful, but he was. So strong and powerful, but so sweet and understanding. The concept of a straight guy able to be both those things had been warring in my mind since I'd met him.

I sat on the chair across from the bed, and just watched him sleep. I knew I was being creepy, but I needed the time to let the factions in my head war with one another.

On one hand, I really wanted him, wanted to let his finger caress my body, like he had begun to do when I freaked out earlier. I wanted to see what it would feel like to have this big, delicious man run his big and oh-so-wonderful hands over my breasts. I might still have been a virgin, I might never have taken a man to my bed, but I'd fantasized enough about it. Shit, since meeting him, I had *only* fantasized about Indi.

I thought of those fantasies as I watched him sleep, and decided to give this another go. Was I playing with fire? Yes. I would probably freak out, but Indi seemed to be okay with it. I decided, if I didn't try, I would probably never get the nerve to do so again.

Before I could chicken out, I removed my top again, and slipped under the covers. I pressed my body up against his, kissing him gently on the lips, until he began to stir.

When his hand came to rub up and down my arms, I kissed him harder, encouraging him to let me in. When he did, the contrast between my heavy kissing, and his gentle caresses was overwhelming.

I crawled on top of him and took his hands, placing them on my breasts like I'd fantasized about. His warm hands moved around my bra, sending a prickling sensation all over me. He explored my upper body, while looking at me with sleepy eyes.

I felt so safe and warm, but also the fire that was inside me was burning brighter and brighter. I lay back next to him. He leaned up on his side, and I took his hand to get him to continue his exploration.

When he leaned over to kiss me, I knew I wanted to feel his mouth where his hands had just been. Indi took the hint quickly, and began to kiss my neck while continuing to rub his hand over me. When he began to use his tongue to explore where his fingers had just been, I felt like the fire had entered my blood.

I felt like I could burst. This man was one hundred percent real. A man who liked women was using his tongue to peruse my entire body. Then, oh my god, when he put his mouth over my covered breast, I thought I'd come unglued. I wanted to scream at him to take my bra off, but I was struck too dumb to do anything other than mumble his name over and over. This wasn't my first time to second base, but I had never felt the tingle of sexual lust I did with Indi.

He slowly lifted himself up to look at me, allowing his muscled stomach to lightly touch mine. "You tell me how far you want to go. When you want to stop, you just have to tell me to stop. Are we clear?" His eyes held his promise, and when I shook my head, he still refused to move. "You need to look me in the eye, and tell me you understand that, Suzie."

I turned back at him, and smiled. "I'll let you know if I want to stop. Now, shut up and get back to work."

He chuckled as his mouth came back down to mine. "I want you so bad," he said, and then let his tongue retrace the path he'd started earlier. When he came to my breasts again, he moved his hands behind my back and undid my bra. I wanted to purr at the release as those beautiful, masculine hands moved under the fabric to touch the sensitive skin beneath. "Oh god," I moaned. He expertly pulled my bra loose, and tossed it across the room, then he let his mouth taste, and then devour my nipples.

If I died right now, I'd be satiated. I couldn't remember a time I'd felt this alive, at least, any time when I wasn't performing in front of a crowded theater. My body trembled as his mouth moved along my body, licking, then nipping in just the right places.

His hands moved to my panties, sliding his fingers underneath the lace. I went rigid before I could stop myself, and put my hand on his. I drew in a breath, just as I started to tremble.

"Fuck," I said out loud. Indi pulled himself off, and sat next to me. "I'm sorry, Indi." I was mortified this was my response once again. "Indi, I... I'm..."

I took a deep breath, and before I could let it out, he said, "You're still a virgin." I shook my head, and the tears began to fall. "Honey, why are you crying?"

He drew me into a hug, and rubbed my back with his hand while kissing my temple. I couldn't stop the waterworks now that they had started, even though I was mortified by them.

When I finally got a grip on myself, I let out a breath, and said, "I didn't think, Indi. I just wanted you so bad, and then when you touched my panties, I freaked out. I didn't want to freak out. I shouldn't have..."

"Shhh," he whispered in my hair. "Baby, I told you we would stop when you needed. I'm just glad you told me. I want to pleasure you. Nothing has to happen, except what you want to happen, okay?" he reminded me again, but it still felt good to hear him say it.

He pulled me back and looked at me. The sweet gesture almost caused the waterworks to start again, but I managed to hold them back. I nodded, and leaned into his embrace.

"If you want, there are other things we could do besides that." All I could do was look at him. My best friends were all gay. My brother was gay. I knew all about gay sex, but in the ways of straight lovemaking, I was more than a little behind.

"Want to try some?"

All I could think of was his mouth, and my desire for it to keep moving around my body. He laid me back down, and let his mouth explore over my body, his hands moving in rhythm to his lips. I knew I moaned a hundred times a second as he explored my breasts, and then down my stomach. When his tongue moved under the lace on my panties, I waited for the same panic to return. When it didn't, I lay back and enjoyed the pleasure he was giving.

He leaned back up to kiss me, and I felt like butter. When we'd crawled back into bed together, he had kept his boxer briefs on, and he let his body move along mine. His erection felt like sheer heaven as it pressed against me.

Even through the clothes we both wore, the feeling was sheer ecstasy. As he moved up and down, I felt for the first time what it must be like to have a man inside of me, and I began to long for it.

I reached down to remove the covering between us, and Indi stopped me. "No, not this time," he said. "This time, it's about exploring each other, letting us both learn and enjoy without the pressure. Okay?" he asked.

I just nodded.

He lowered himself back down and returned to letting our bodies rub against each other. I grabbed him and pulled him down, so his entire weight rested on me, and began kissing the hard muscles of his neck and shoulders.

It was then that I remembered all the lessons I'd learned from my gay friends, and realized there were a *lot* of things I could do to him that didn't involve fucking. I pushed him off me and straddled him. Now, *this* was going to be fun.

# Indi

The woman hit every sexual button in me. One minute we were strolling companionably together, and the next thing I knew, she wanted to go to bed. I did what I could to be a good man. I hated that others of my gender would take advantage of a woman, and if I encountered it, I would have no problem sending a man like that to an early grave. But no matter how much I wanted to be sensitive, I was never, and I meant never, going to say no to having this woman consent to being in my bed, with us naked and squirming around on each other.

Suzie's body was perfect. Her breasts were full and beautiful. Her muscular frame was small and delicately built. I could almost taste her. It was all I could do not to just jump on her, and hump her like the caveman I could feel myself becoming.

That primitive part of me warred with the desire to be as sensual to her as I could possibly be. I knew from previous conversations, she had not had much experience sexually, so I was damn sure if it was the last thing I ever did, I would take my time and give her pleasure. Besides, I knew trust was important, so she had to be in charge.

I made her look me in the eye, and tell me she understood, and that was good, because when I touched her underwear, she freaked. I had a suspicion she might be a virgin, but things between us had been so wacky, I hadn't had the chance to ask her. When she started to cry, I felt my heart stop. All I wanted to do was pull her into my arms, and protect her from the world.

If I could go back in time and beat the shit out of the person who had done this to her, I would gladly do so. I doubted he even thought about it, but damn, he'd screwed her up.

The idea that I'd be interested in doing something besides fucking, seemed to surprise her. That actually threw me. Why wouldn't I enjoy all the other stuff? Don't get me wrong, I loved that too, but the other stuff was every bit as exciting. Suzie's body turned me on in every way. Why wouldn't I want to explore it?

When I began touching her again, something seemed to change inside of her. Before I knew it, I was on my back, and Suzie was straddling me, and looking down at me with a wicked grin. I couldn't help smiling back. I liked playful Suzie a hell of a lot better than insecure Suzie.

*Let the games begin.*

Suzie leaned over and kissed me, but nothing about that kiss was gentle. She buried her tongue in my mouth, exploring with intensity.

She kissed my neck, and then whispered in my ear, "I'm about to rock your world, Indi Freemont."

I was already hard, but my dick somehow got harder with her comment. Was it a threat? God, whatever it was, it was hot as hell, and I wanted her more than I thought I could.

She bit my neck just on the pulse point, and I'd swear she was trying to give me a hickey. She moved her mouth down to my pectoral, and let her tongue glide over my nipples. I sucked in a breath, and she looked up at me just as she bit down on one. I sucked in another breath, then moaned. I felt her chuckle against my stomach, and I thought I would crumble under the sexual tension that feeling sent to my groin.

After nipping and sucking in all the right places, she let her mouth move down to my stomach and then sat up. She was smiling that evil smile again. Her ass began to move up and down, stimulating me, and I thought I was going to come right then and there.

"Oh, my god, Suzie, I fucking love that," I purred. That made her grin even more sadistically. She moved down and found me with her mouth. I could feel her hot breath through my boxers, and you'd think I'd never had a blow job from the way I reacted to her.

I moaned and arched, completely under her spell. She lifted off and looked at me.

"Take your boxers off," she demanded, and I complied as quickly as I could.

When I finally returned her gaze, she went back down on me, sucking me into the back of her mouth, and making me squirm and moan loudly with pleasure.

"Suzie!" I put my hand over her head, and said, "I... I'm going to come I... I can't stop."

She pulled off of me as my release gripped me. She leaned over, and smiled. "That was intense," she said after a moment.

I could tell she was startled. "Are you okay? I should've stopped, but I just couldn't. I'm so sorry," I told her again.

"For what?" she asked teasingly. "I did what I wanted to do. It isn't always about the guy, Indi!" Then, she moved up my body with cat-like movements, and took my mouth with hers.

"Fuck," was all I could say.

She laughed again and moved to get up.

I grabbed her, and pulled her back to me. Now it was my turn. She looked at me, confused, but slowly realization came to her.

While she was gazing at me with those doe eyes, I said, "I want to make you feel like that too. Do you trust me?"

The confident Suzie was still there, but it warred with the Suzie who was inexperienced and afraid.

"Let me show you the pleasure," I all but begged. "I promise, if you are uncomfortable, I'll stop."

She looked at me, desire and curiosity in her expression, and nodded.

I grinned, and let my mouth explore her body, getting her as turned on as I could. She was moaning as I let my mouth explore her breasts, while my hands massaged her through the silky fabric she still had on.

'Oh, god," she murmured as my mouth moved down her torso.

"Can I take these off?" I asked, and she looked at me and nodded again.

I slowly took them down and then beheld the beautiful body that was before me. "You are the most beautiful woman," I said.

Her eyes continued to watch me as I let my mouth continue its exploration. I kissed her hips, and let my tongue explore her thighs, giving her time to get used to my being in that intimate space.

When she moaned and called my name, I knew I could take this to the next level. I let my tongue explore her. I looked into her eyes, watching for any discomfort. When there was none, I changed the motion of my tongue against her, causing her to moan.

I'd loved Suzie's attention on me earlier, but watching her while I caused her to feel the same ecstasy was euphoric.

I could see that she was about to crest, and felt giddy, knowing I was the first man to ever cause her to have that kind of sensation. I watched as the feeling came on her, and she writhed in pleasure and excitement.

She was panting and breathing hard as the moment overtook her. Her eyes were wide as the feeling finally passed, and I smiled at her, before coming up to kiss her.

"Oh, god," she finally said. "*That* was fucking amazing."

I laughed in spite of myself. "Yeah, it was."

We lay in each other's arms as she snuggled against me.

"I didn't know what I was missing. Vibrators are no comparison," she said with a chuckle.

"I think as we learn each other's body, it'll only get better, but that comes with trust," I said as I kissed the back of her delicious neck. Just then, her stomach growled. "Hungry?" I asked.

She snickered. "Yeah, maybe a little," she said. "All I've had to eat since lunch was you."

"Just a mere snack," I teased her.

"Do you want to order something? Pizza maybe?" I asked.

She just nodded, and said, "Whatever. Mostly, I just want to stay like this."

"Deal," I said.

I leaned over and found my phone, and the number for our favorite pizza. "Anything you don't like on it?" I asked.

"Just none of the nasty stuff like dead fish or pineapple," she said.

"Canadian Bacon?" I asked

"Sure," she shrugged.

I ordered the pizza, then came back and snuggled her against me. "You are the most incredible woman ever. I love your body, especially here," I said as I gently moved my hand over her boobs.

She turned around and looked at me. "I don't have a lot of expecrience with men, but I can tell you have a pretty nice piece of meat down there." Then, she smiled that naughty smile at me again, and I felt my heart melt a bit.

"Meat is it?" I asked, and went in for the tickle. She was screaming and laughing at the same time, when my bedroom door flung open.

"What the hell?" a voice asked.

I turned over and looked at the door to see a pissed-off Denim. Suzie quickly pulled what little covers were still on the bed over her. "What are you doing, Denim?" I asked.

"You... you..." he stuttered. "What are you doing? Suzie, I thought you left."

I threw the pillow at him and told him to get the fuck out! He shut the door with an expression of utter shock.

I yelled at the door as it closed, "Hey, there's pizza coming! Pay for it!"

"Fuck you," was all I heard.

"Um..." Suzie said, "...maybe we better go clear that up."

I wasn't really wanting to get up. The only thing I wanted to do was keep this beautiful body wrapped up in mine.

"Shit, I guess you're right," I grudgingly agreed. "Fuck, sometimes having family really cramps my style."

Suzie laughed. "Ain't that the truth."

# Suzie

We both threw on clothes and came downstairs. Denim was sitting in a chair, appearing both confused and a little shocked. I sat on the sofa next to him, and reached over to pat his knee.

"Are you okay, hon?" I asked. He shook his head, but continued staring at the coffee table in front of him.

I glanced over at Indi, and shrugged as discreetly as I could.

"Denim, buddy?" Indi pushed.

Next thing I know, Denim looked at me and a blush rose up his face. "Suzie, I saw more of you than I ever wanted to," he said.

He looked back at Indi, and said, "I wouldn't have burst in like that if I had known you had Suzie in your room, and that she was a *consenting* adult!"

"Why the fuck wouldn't she be consenting?" Indi asked with indignation. "You all have to stop making assumptions about me, just because I'm straight. I do have *some* damned integrity when it comes to women. *Shit*, besides, wasn't it you and Clay setting us up in the first place?"

Then, Indi stood up and went into the kitchen.

Denim was appropriately chastised. "Go talk to him. We've all made assumptions about him, but I'm sure it hurts worse coming from his brother."

I wandered back upstairs to give Denim and Indi some space. I hated that Indi was feeling stereotyped. It wasn't fair. He was one of the most empathetic men I'd ever met. Well, *straight* men, that was. Some of my gay friends were more sensitive than me, but I knew Indi was something special when it came to the typical guy. If you added on top of that he was all but a jock, well, it made him extra special.

It took a while for Indi to come back to the bedroom. Despite it still being early, I had drifted off while waiting. When I woke up, he was sitting on the bed staring at the wall.

"What's wrong?" I asked, while stretching.

Indi's expression registered frustration and a bit of anger. It took him a moment to find his words, which I could see him struggling with.

"I know there's a lot of guys who are bad men. I know you have to watch your back when you're with those guys, but I'm not one of them, and I don't hang out with guys like that. I like you, Suzie. I like you a lot, maybe more than I've ever liked a woman at this point in a relationship, but I can't continue paying for the actions of other men."

At this, he sighed, and turned back toward the wall.

I sat up then, and crawled onto my knees. "I can't promise I won't forget and accidentally compare you to other men, or the one guy from my past who put me into the place where I don't really trust straight guys, but I can try." Indi looked back over at me, and I could see my words had registered, so I continued, "I haven't trusted any straight men since I was sixteen... This is hard, and unfortunately, you are the first guy to break through the walls... I just can't promise I'm going to be okay. I already told you, there is a lot of baggage here."

I couldn't stop the tears that escaped me. Indi used his thumb to wipe them away, then pulled me into his arms. "So, this is going to be an effort on both our parts, huh?"

I knew I was feeling vulnerable enough at this point that I could bawl like a baby, so I elected to shrug instead of answering. I leaned into him and drew from his strength. We sat like that for a long time, before I leaned up and kissed his cheek.

"You already took me further than any man ever has. I'll work on it, I promise." He smiled at me, and I noticed a couple dimples that had escaped my attention before.

"I guess the least I can do is try to help you work through it when your past experiences with men get confused with me."

I couldn't help myself, I had to kiss him again. This was the sweetest, most patient and loving man ever. How did I get so lucky?

The kiss started as sweet, and then slowly became more. We spent the next few hours exploring each other's bodies. I decided I loved sex, at least sex with

Indi, and thanked whatever deities were responsible for our coming together.

# Indi

By the time we got back to the living room, the pizza we ordered was sitting on the kitchen counter, and it was cold.

A small price to pay, considering I got to be with an amazing woman like Suzie while waiting. Denim was nowhere to be seen, and I assumed that he'd probably gone out after our confrontation.

I understood why Suzie was afraid of me, but I certainly didn't get why my own brother, who knew me better than anyone else on the planet, was afraid of how I'd treat her.

When he'd burst into my room, I could tell he had assumed the worst, and I'd be damned if I was going to let that pass a second time.

I laid into him pretty hard after Suzie had left the room, and he just sat there with his face down. Fuck, if that didn't just piss me off more. Denim knew I wasn't that kind of man. What the hell would make him assume I was?

When he didn't respond, I headed upstairs, and finding Suzie asleep, I just sat on the edge of the bed, giving myself time to think.

When she woke up, the conversation about coming to terms with her past was what we needed, and the sex after was worth taking the time to spell things out.

Suzie and I sat across from each other, eating our cold pizza, and making eyes at one another. This woman was the right fit in every way. I had assumed she was a *fill-every-minute-with-talk* kind of person, but apparently, she was comfortable being together in silence.

When we finished the pizza, we sat on the sofa watching some crappy TV. Finally, around nine she got up, stretched and announced she was headed back to her place. "You don't wanna stay over?" I asked.

She leaned over and kissed me, then took my lower lip in her teeth in a sexy, teasing way. "Absence makes the heart grow fonder, they say." She chuckled.

"Fuck them, my heart is pretty fond right now," I replied, earning me what I was beginning to understand was Suzie's *Broadway* laugh.

"I need to get home and get some actual sleep tonight," she said. "I have back-to-back performances for the next six days, so I can't afford to start the week dragging butt. After I'm done, I would love to spend the night with you." She confirmed her statement by another deep and sexy kiss.

Of course, I was hard as a rock all over again. "Suzie, you are doing this on purpose."

She grinned a naughty grin. "Six days is a long time. I just don't want you to forget me while I'm gone," she teased.

It was my turn to laugh out loud. "Like that is humanly possible. Suzie, there is nothing forgettable about you!"

She all but purred as she kissed me one last time, got up, and headed for the door.

"Hey, can I drive you home?" I asked.

She chuckled. "No. I can get home quicker using the subway."

I couldn't argue with her. The traffic, even on a Sunday night, was still pretty thick. So, I got up and walked over to the door where she stood.

"I already miss you," I said, kind of whining.

She chuckled again, then in typical Suzie Diva style, she said, "Good," opened the door, and disappeared down the road.

My last thought as I watched her walk away was that I'd never meet another woman like Suzie Fisher.

# Suzie

I loved what I did for a living. I knew the world was full of people who coveted my place, but the six-day stretch between when I last saw Indi until today was sheer torture.

When I was lamenting the death of my beloved Lydia, I substituted her for him, and the tears were real, and much more painful than they had been before. I had acted the part almost daily for over a year, and I never really understood what Beta would've felt losing the love of her life, until I had Indi as a comparison.

Part of me connected with Beta on a totally different level that week, and naturally, the reviews showed it. One review for the *Times* was especially on point:

*"The emotional impact displayed by Suzie Fisher as she lamented the loss of her soul mate, Lydia, was especially*

*heartbreaking. Unlike other actors on the stage, she seems to become more embedded with her character as time goes on."*

Little did they know, it was the lament of one, a man, and two, just having to be away from him for this show. I was sure the reviews wouldn't have been so kind, if they knew that tidbit of information.

Finally, at the end of the stretch, I was determined to go see Indi the first chance I got, but instead, I went home the last night and crashed. I slept a full sixteen hours, which wasn't all that uncommon for me. These shows were both emotionally and physically challenging, and when I gave it my all, I tended to need a bit of downtime to recoup.

When I finally came back to the living, there were three texts from Indi.

First, *"I went to see your show this week. Damn, I'm not worthy of you."*

Second, *"I miss you so much it hurts all over. When are you available? Yes, I'm pathetic, sue me."*

Third, *"Don't avoid me, because I'm a pathetic Suzie Fisher groupie. I'm only sort of dangerous, and in a totally,*

*totally, good way."* This was followed by a mischievous-looking emoji.

It was the middle of the afternoon, but I decided to call him anyway, just in case he could pick up. He answered on the second ring, "Hey."

"Hey," I replied back. "What are you wearing?"

He chuckled in a deep, very sexy way, and replied, "I can't have phone sex with you right now. I'm kind of at work."

"Humm," I moaned, intentionally trying to be naughty. "That makes it so *much* more fun."

"You have to stop that right now," he replied. "You're all I've thought about for the past week, and I have a meeting in fifteen minutes. I can't afford to show up with a ha... well, with my package sticking out," he corrected.

I laughed so hard, I thought I'd pee myself. This guy totally pushed my happy buttons. "What are you doing tonight?" I asked, before falling onto my back, and immediately imagining him lying on top of me.

"I hope I'm spending time with you," he said.

"Good, that's what I'm hoping as well. Want me to wear my Beta costume?"

There was a silence on the other end of the line, then I heard him cuss, "Damn it, Suzie, I have a meeting, remember? Okay, got to go. I am totally going to have to wander around my office thinking about hairy old men, or something!"

Again, I couldn't help laughing at the thought of Indi trying to hide his hard-on. "Then it's settled. I'll see you at your place around sixish, and I'll bring Beta along for the ride... And it's going to be a very nice ride."

"Shit," was all I heard, before he hung up on me.

I should have gone pee before I called him, but I had no idea he was going to make me laugh that hard. Would tonight be the night we went all the way? It seemed like that should be something more monumental, but the feminist in me said that I was being a Victorian snit, and should get over the whole damned thing.

The romantic in me, however, wanted this to be something that I remembered fondly, and even though I was sure I wanted Indi to be my first in that way too, I wanted it to be special for both of us.

When I came out of the bathroom, I got online and looked up romantic getaways, and found a place in Martha's Vineyard. I'd ask him tonight if he was open to a drive this weekend. There was something wrong with the theater, and they had to make repairs, so we had been given a couple of days off the following weekend, which was odd. I also took it as a sign. The extra time off meant we could make this something great for both of us.

Of course, I was starving, so I got my shower and ran out to the grocery store. I decided I could cook something special for Indi tonight, if Denim could let me in early, and then I could seduce him with my... wait, I couldn't cook. That was my brother. Shit. I picked the phone up immediately, and called Clay.

"Hey, girlfriend, what's going on?" he answered, skipping the traditional greeting like he always did.

"Hi, honey. I need advice."

"Whatever can I do for you, my love?"

"I want to bring a romantic dinner to Indi. We want to *stay in*, if you know what I mean, but I can't cook. What do you suggest?"

I could hear Clay speaking to someone in the background. I assumed it was either Denim, or someone at a photoshoot he was at.

When he came back on the line, he said, "No problem, Denim and I can have something for you. We are at a photoshoot together, but will be home around four, then we have to be back for night shots after six."

"Clay, no offense, but you and Denim cook worse than I do."

Clay laughed out loud. I heard someone in the background call him back to the shoot, and he quickly said, "I promise it'll be delicious and sexy, and neither Denim nor I will get our hands dirty with the process."

"Oh, Honey, thank you so much," I said as he hung up, still chuckling.

I figured I would wait until after five to show up, so the two of them had some alone time before their next shoot. I knew from being in the back room that when models had to be all over each other half dressed, it could often end up with them having sex between shoots. *And good for them*, I thought. Now that I finally had a man who turned me on that much, I hoped we'd be having some hot sex every chance we got as well.

When I got to the townhouse, Clay and Denim were headed out the door, but Clay ran over to the refrigerator and pointed out several boxes of what appeared to be different Italian dishes. I asked if Italian was sexy.

Clay smiled and said, "Does it matter?"

"Fuck, no," I replied. "At this point, I'm randy enough that hamburgers and fries are sexy to me." Both Clay and Denim laughed as they headed out the door. I called after them, "Hey, what do I owe you?"

"Oh, nothing," Clay said. "We swiped that from the caterer. They brought dinner for those of us who were supposed to stay on between shoots. Of course, most models don't eat anything with that many carbs, so there was plenty left over."

"You are sweethearts." I blew a kiss at them as they left. "Don't feel like you have to rush home tonight," I said as the door shut. I could still hear their laughter through the door.

I was totally nervous. I hadn't told Indi I was coming over early, but I wanted to surprise him and turn him on, so he'd put those incredible hands back on me again.

I climbed into my Beta outfit. I had to make sure I didn't mess it up, because I'd be murdered by the costume department if I did. I'd swiped it, knowing I was taking my life in my own hands. Of course, if it got the reaction I hoped it would, death would be a small price to pay.

I decided to leave the food in the boxes, thinking if I played my cards right, we wouldn't need that for a while.

When I came out of the bathroom, Indi was standing in the living room, shocked to see me. Being in my Beta outfit must have stirred my sexual confidence, because I bent over and showed my posterior.

When I looked back, all the color had drained from Indi's face, and the erection he had worked to hide earlier was clearly visible under his khakis.

I sauntered over, rubbed my hand over the lump, and said in a sultry voice, "Are you... happy to see me?"

The next thing I knew, Indi had me up against him, and it was clear as day how happy he was to see me. The kiss was all want and need. His hands were all over me, pulling me to him as his mouth devoured mine. I knew there was nothing soft or gentle about what was going to happen next. I waited for the old fear to surface, but it wasn't there. In fact, all that was there for me was my mirror image of his desire.

I pulled away, putting my hand up to stop him from coming near. Executing as many of my "Beta-like characteristics" as I could, I let the little outfit fall from my body, placing it aside. Even in the heat of the moment, I was afraid of the wrath of Mrs. Cummings, the costume director.

When I turned around, I was naked from the waist up. Indi moaned from where he stood. Seeing the control I had over him turned me on even more, and I moved my body up toward his, forcing him to keep his hands off. I let my hand trail around him, moving up and down, stroking, prodding, and playing with him as I went.

Finally, I forced him onto his knees, and in a way that was completely uncharacteristic of me, I stripped everything off but my stockings and pressed myself to his mouth, which he took with pleasure. I almost melted when his tongue moved over me.

Indi slowly took my stockings down and pressed his tongue to my center.

I embraced his head, and rocked against his tongue, enjoying the sensation of his mouth on me, and the feeling that I was somehow controlling how we made love.

It was exciting—no—exhilarating to feel so much power.

He used his tongue to explore me, fill me with pleasure, and I was quickly becoming a wet noodle of need. When he moved his fingers up me, and used them to open me, pulling me into his mouth, I moaned so loud it was almost a scream.

As he held me to his face, I began to crest, the sensation overtaking my entire body.

He pulled back from me then, and locking eye contact with me, smiled slyly and began to move back up my body letting his tongue explore every part of me as he did. "Let's go to bed," he whispered. The stubble from a day of work slightly rubbed against my ear, and a shiver started at the top of my head, and settled into the part of my body still wet with his saliva.

I wasn't ready to give up control, even though my body was putty at this point, so I grabbed his hand, then slowly pulled him up the stairs, and toward his bedroom.

When we arrived, I pushed him onto the bed, and climbed on top of him. I ground myself on his cock, watching him squirm then arch with pleasure. "I'm going to come if you don't stop," he exclaimed.

"Good," I said with a wicked smile.

Then I crawled down him, kissing his nipples, biting just a little too hard, which caused him to suck in a breath, and cry a bit at the same time.

I nibbled down his chest and his tight abs, the perfect six-pack that turned me on even more.

When I found his erection, I put my hand around the base, but before I took him in my mouth, I looked back up to him. His eyes were on me, and the look of complete surrender caused me to moan. I kept watching him as I took him into my mouth and moved my tongue.

He moaned so loud, I automatically thought he was going to come then, but instead I heard him say, "Oh god, Suzie, I need you so much."

I pulled off and asked how much he needed me.

He leaned up on his elbows and said, "I need you more than air right now."

That was what I wanted to hear, and I sucked him back into my mouth. It gagged me, as I suspected it would, but when he all but screamed in response, the sound of his pleasure was totally worth it.

I sucked him up and down, letting my tongue explore him each time, before I took him into the back of my throat, only gagging a couple of times.

When I could tell he was getting used to the pleasure, I took it up a few notches, until he yelled, "Suzie! Suzie!" over and over again, then, "I'm going to come."

Watching him come made me feel so strong. Not only could I give him pleasure, but I could let him give the same pleasure to me. The feeling that I had that much power, sent chills through me.

I fell down on the bed next to him, and he quickly went into the bathroom, only to emerge a moment later. When he lay next to me, he nuzzled his nose into my hair saying, "I have never met a woman who turns me on like you do, Suzie."

I jokingly replied, "You mean *Beta* turns you on."

He rose up on an elbow and looked at me, saying, "No, Suzie turns me on. That was all you. Just because you were in a sexy costume, and pretending to be someone else on stage, doesn't change the fact that I'm attracted to you, and only you."  Then, he leaned over and kissed me again.

His kiss was quickly becoming more heated when I pushed him back, and laughed. "Wait, there's food. You need nourishment if I'm to get everything out of you I have planned."

He gave me an inquisitive expression, "What do you have planned?"

"You'll see," I said, and I pulled him up, barely giving him time to pull on some boxers, before pulling him back down the stairs.

"Honey," he said, "I love seeing you like this, but I don't want my brother to walk in and see you in all your glory."

I laughed, and said, "No worries. Your brother knows we need some alone time, and he and Clay are working tonight."

"Mmm," he moaned, and brought me into a hug, saying, "Then, maybe I will want to use these as my plate." His mouth found my nipples again.

"Oh, god! That felt so good," I said, but I pushed him back in a playful way. "Eat first, sex later."

He held on nonetheless, and whined, "Do we have to?"

"I promise to make it up to you," I said, shivering as his mouth moved across my breast again.

He leaned away and smiled at me. "I'm going to hold you to that promise."

I put my panties on, then went into the kitchen to get the food out and warm it up. As we waited, Indi sat at the counter. I turned to him, and said, "I've been thinking about going all the way." He cocked an eyebrow at me, but didn't say anything. I was becoming self-conscious, so I looked away, but continued to talk,

"I want it to be special, but I already know I want it to be with you. You've already been my first in so many ways. I want you to be my first in this as well." I wasn't able to find the nerve to look back at him.

Before I knew it, two strong arms were around me, and he was kissing me on my neck. "I feel really honored," he said. "I promise to make it as special as I can."

I turned back into him, and I couldn't explain why that made me want to cry. We hugged until the microwave buzzer went off, and I curled out of his arms to take the food out.

"I looked at a resort in Martha's Vineyard for the weekend. No offense, but if we are going to go all the way, I'd prefer to do it in a place where I know your brother won't accidentally walk in."

He laughed and pulled me back into an embrace. "My parents own a cottage in the Hamptons that they hardly ever use. If you want to go away, I'll have their maid service get it ready for us. It's pretty secluded there, and has easy access to the beach. Does that sound okay?"

Again, I felt tears sting my eyes. He was taking care of me, even when this was my idea, and the sweetness behind it almost turned me into a blubbering idiot. I just leaned into his big, handsome, strong body, and nodded into his chest.

After several minutes, I felt I had managed to get past my tears, and I leaned back to get the food plated.

He relaxed back into his place at the counter to watch me. I was so self-conscious at this point that I didn't dare look back at him, lest the tears came back.

I plopped the food unceremoniously in front of him, and sat next to him, suddenly aware of the fact that I was naked, except for my panties, which made me even more self-conscious. I started to get up, and Indi's hand went to my shoulder and lightly held me there.

"If you are having second thoughts, we can stop and let this rest until another day," he said.

Then, the tears fell, despite everything I tried to do to stop them. "You are just being too nice, and I'm a blubbering idiot," I said through the tears.

He smiled and gathered me back into his arms. "You don't have to hide your tears from me, Dear One. They don't scare me. Watching you fight them—that often looks like you are unsure about stuff, and that *does* scare me. So, let's make a deal. You let the tears come when they need to, and I'll promise to be here for you when they do. Deal?" he asked.

I just nodded, and said, "Okay, enough stupid tears. Let's eat, so we can get back to the good stuff."

He laughed, reached over, and kissed me before I could take a bite. He looked down at my exposed breasts, and sighed. "I fully support that proposal!"

# Indi

As we lay in bed sexually satiated, Suzie looked over and asked. "Where the hell did 'Indi' come from?"

The randomness of the question caused me to laugh out loud, and I looked over, asking, "Where did that question come from?"

"I was just thinking how strange yours and your brother's names are. Why Indi?"

I chuckled, and before answering, said, "I'm not sure how I feel about my girlfriend thinking about my brother after we just had sex, but..."

At first, I didn't realize I had called her my girlfriend, but the way Suzie tensed, forced me to reevaluate my words before going on.

When I realized what I'd said, I looked over, afraid of what her reaction would be. "I know I kind of jumped the gun a bit on that statement, huh?" I asked.

Suzie just nodded, trying to look nonchalant.

"Okay, now that it's out," I said with a sigh. "Let's talk about it. I wasn't seeing anyone when we met, and I don't really want to see anyone but you. So, can I call you my girlfriend?"

Suzie smiled and blushed with apparent shyness. That look on her face was very uncharacteristic, so of course, it sent shockwaves all over my body.

She nodded, then leaned over to kiss me. "I like being your girlfriend. It's kinda my first time with that too."

I continued to forget all the stuff this amazing woman had lost out on. If only I could go back in time and beat that pipsqueak into a pulp...

"So, it's settled. We're girlfriend and boyfriend." The comment made me feel childish, and I almost made some snarky comment about how we should've passed notes with a "circle yes or no," but my instincts told me that Suzie wouldn't find the same humor in that as I did. This really was a first for her, and unlike those who didn't have damaging high-school relationships, she had experienced things very differently.

She curled up into my arms then, and whether the comment was childish or not, the feeling of contentment that I had even an ounce of belonging to that woman, caused my heart to soar.

"Now that we're official, I want to know about your name, Indi," Suzie insisted.

"My name came from Indigo. That's the color they used to dye blue-jean material back when my grandfather and great-grandfather ran a blue-jean factory here in town. Something about that caused my parents to want to use our past as a way to name us. I'm Indigo, the color, and Denim is the type of material we made. Stupid, huh?" I felt self-conscious all of a sudden.

Suzie turned to me with a smile. "It is strange, but I like it, and Indi makes me think of Indiana Jones, who I secretly had a crush on when I was a little girl."

Seeing a dreamy look on her face, I couldn't help harassing her. "Ew, you have a thing for old men?"

Suzie, picking up on my teasing, elbowed me in the ribs and said, "He wasn't old when the films were made, and I was a little girl, so everyone was old to me."

I laughed, and said, "So, do I remind you of Indiana Jones in name only, or should I go buy a fedora?"

Her smile was feline when she looked back at me, and said, "I won't tell you to wear one or not, but if you happened to be wearing one, it might or might not have the same effect on me as my Beta costume did on you tonight."

My mind got lost for a moment as I thought of what that reaction might lead to, and I couldn't help wondering about where I could get my hands on one of those before the weekend.

When I rolled back toward her, the feline smile was still on her face. "You're thinking about it, aren't you?"

I nodded, and the same grin she sported came to my face. "So, when can you get away for a weekend?" I asked.

"They're doing repairs, so the theater will be shut down over next weekend. I'm available after Friday night."

"Perfect," I said, and curled into her as we both fell asleep.

I'd slept with several women over the years, but having Suzie Fisher tucked into me as we spooned, was pure pleasure. I know it's a *cliché* to say we fit together perfectly, but *cliché* or not, that was exactly how it felt. I wasn't someone who liked to cuddle either, but having her against me was so comfortable, so right, that I didn't dare move. We fell asleep this way, and when I woke the following morning, she was still snuggled into me.

I wanted to jump up and down screaming to the world that this woman wanted me, and she was snuggling with me, and only me. No one else had ever had her, and she was going to let me be her very first.

I knew that sounded chauvinistic, and part of me was embarrassed about that, but the fact was, the happy feeling had a lot more to do with knowing she trusted me more than anyone else. That made me special, and it made what we had even more special. That was worth all the money in the world to me.

Suzie stirred, probably because I was all but vibrating with happiness. I had to pee like a racehorse, so I managed to disentangle myself. When I came back, she was still fast asleep. Seeing I only had ten minutes before my alarm announced that I had to get ready for work, I turned it off and went to take my shower.

The woman slept like a log, so I managed to get ready without waking her, and was going to slip out the door, but I just couldn't leave without kissing that beautiful mouth, all puckered up with sleep. When I kissed her, she stirred, and smiled up at me.

"Leaving already?"

"Yeah," I said with a sigh. "I have to go to work."

"Are you going to work out?" she said.

"No. I wanted to spend as much time with you as I could, so I didn't get up in time."

"That's sweet," she said, and turned back into her pillow.

"I'm going to go, sweetheart," I said against her cheek. "

She just sighed, and I was sure she was asleep again. I couldn't help smiling at how beautiful she was, lying in my sheets. I had to admit, I had it really bad if the sight of her in my bed made me go soft inside.

I shook my head as I exited the bedroom. I could only hope if I was this close to falling in love with Suzie Fisher, that her feelings were similar. If not, I was going to have one hell of a heartache when, or if, she ever broke up with me.

# Suzie

Indi picked me up on Saturday morning earlier, than I would usually wake up, but I had told him I wanted to go ASAP, so we could enjoy the weekend as much as possible. As we drove the four and a half hours to get to his parents' cabin, I slept.

When we finally got to the cottage, it was just before noon, and I was famished. I stretched and yawned, and my first question was, "Do we have any food?"

Indi laughed. "Yeah, I had the maid service stock some of the basics, but if you want more than cereal, we'd better go shopping first."

I stretched again, and said, "I'm all for cereal, then we can see what happens from there."

We unloaded the car and ate a bowl of *Peanut Butter Crunch* on the front porch; it was apparently Indi's and Denim's favorite cereal. The cottage looked out over the beach and the Atlantic. It was a beautiful spot. I'd been to the Hamptons several times, and had yet to stay in a place that actually faced the water.

"So," I said, trying to sound nonchalant. "Just how wealthy is your family?"

Indi looked around our surroundings, and chuckled. "My great-grandpa had this built here in the 1920s. Admittedly, he was wealthier than we are, but we had enough that we didn't have to sell this for the money. My parents do rent it out from time to time, but they're really picky about who they allow to rent it, so it mostly sits empty."

"That's a shame," I said as I looked out at the view, then back inside at the quaint furnishings. "It really is a nice place."

Indi smiled. "Pretty romantic?" he asked, a sly grin sneaking up on his face.

"Pretty romantic," I said as I cuddled into his arms, almost spilling his cereal. "Let's go make love." I said it more to trip him up than anything, but he surprised me by putting his cereal down and pulling me into his lap.

I giggled, but he had me in a position that I couldn't get away from, and then began tickling me. "Indi! Indi, stop!" I laughed. He stopped and pulled me around to look at him.

"You are so beautiful, Suzie. I want to make love to you all day and all night."

I leaned in for a kiss, chaste at first, but he immediately turned it to more, letting his tongue slip into my mouth and begin playing with mine.

I moaned under his kiss, and as it became more intense, I arched myself into him, his strong arms holding me gently in his lap.

I felt the tug of his crotch on my buttocks, and I knew he was feeling excited about the prospect of what I'd proposed. All I could think of was that he was going to be my first. I was going to get to give this amazing man pleasure, and he would always be the first man to touch me in that way.

Immediately, I thought of the boy who had tried to be first, and the exhilaration of the moment turned sour. I didn't want to hurt Indi, but I had to pull away. I tried desperately not to let him see the revulsion, but apparently, I was not as good at acting as I thought I was.

"Suzie," he asked, concern etched on his face. "What's wrong?"

I pulled myself off his lap and went to sit across from him on the porch rail. "Nothing, it was just moving faster than I was ready for. I know we came up here for..." I wasn't sure how to phrase it without discounting how important the event was to me, so I was at a loss for words.

"Suzie," Indi said. "We don't have to do anything you don't want. I'm just happy—*more* than happy to be here with you, and have you in my arms."

I sighed. The man was too nice, too sweet, and his concern truly made things different for me. It gave me the power to be strong, and not feel like I wanted to run away.

I decided to be honest with him. "I still have that son of a bitch in my head, Indi. I was just thinking about how I was going to give myself to you, to be yours, and that I'd be able to give you pleasure, when my mind went back to that... that... *ass!*" I said, frustrated with myself, and really angry once again at the guy who'd tried to rape me, and did steal my innocence.

"Sweetheart," Indi said as he came over, and squatted in front of me. "Let's let things just happen. If it's the right time, we'll both know it. If it isn't, let's not push it, okay?"

I was ready to cry again, and I truly didn't want to spoil the moment by blubbering on his shoulder.

"Okay," I said. "We've given the shithead enough of our time today. Let's go shopping, and then spend some time on the beach. I know it's still too cold to swim, but it's warm enough for a picnic."

Indi agreed, and we went to put our bowls in the sink. I grabbed Indi as he was preparing to walk away. I hugged him tight. "I'm sorry this isn't easier. I want it to be easier, I really do."

Indi just kissed my head. "You need to stop worrying so much. Seriously, we will both know it's time when it's time."

We walked hand-in-hand out to the car and got in. My butt was still sore from the long drive here, but I knew I couldn't survive on cereal alone. We shopped and bought way more food than we could eat during the weekend, but we were having so much fun I thought it got easier to just go crazy and enjoy the moment.

People assumed we were married. What a crock. People in New York never assumed a couple were married, unless there was a ring, or maybe if they were bickering. But after the third person asked us, we both silently agreed to pretend we were. At one point, Indi made up that we were the Beckermans, Mr. and Mrs. Beckerman. That worked fine, until he forgot our name halfway into a conversation, and I had to help him out mid-sentence.

I teased him when we got back into the car that the first thing you have to remember when you're acting, or lying in this case, is your fake name.

He just chuckled. "That, My Dear, is why I never lasted as an actor. Remembering lines isn't my forte."

"You make a good agent, though, right?" I asked.

"I make an excellent agent, but I make a lousy salesman, and unfortunately, I have not done so great at attracting clients." He sighed. "Oh, well. I have several people who are doing well. Being an agent is like everything else in this business. You're either lucky, or you work your ass off, until you finally get where you're going."

"The word on the street is you saved a chorus girl, whose dad was about to flog the director, because her competition let the cat out of the bag."

He looked at me funny. "How did you hear about that?"

"My director is friends with Joel Silverstein. When he heard we were dating, he told the story to the entire cast. Broadway's a small world. Gossip flies like we are in a small town."

Indi chuckled. "That's an interesting story. Joel ended up firing the girl who'd set it all up. He is not a patient man when it comes to that kind of stuff."

I nodded. "I've heard he's tough. So, why haven't you tried to recruit me?"

It was Indi's turn to look at me funny, before returning his gaze back to the road. "Why would I? You're already a major success. Besides, it doesn't feel right for me to try to recruit you while we're dating." He looked back over at me and winked. "If I had to choose between being your agent and dating you, I much prefer the dating part."

I just shook my head. "You're different than most of the people I know, Indi. I usually can't get in a room with an agent without them trying to convince me to come to their firm. Why are you so laid back about it?"

"Like I said, I prefer us being on a personal basis, not professional." He thought for a moment. "Suzie, I don't have to depend on the money I make. I'm far from wealthy, but I have all I need. I'm an agent, because I love being an agent. I love my clients, even though more than a few of them are insane." He chuckled.

"If you have some friends or acquaintances that need an agent, please send them my way. If not, then that's cool too. Mostly, I want to get to know you, touch you, wake up beside you. Your acting career is phenomenal, and your level of talent is breathtaking, so I intend to see everything you're in. I'll even be happy to help your agent out with things that pop up, if you promise not to tell my boss, but you need to know, I want you. Not Beta." He thought for a moment, then corrected himself, "Not that I mind Beta..."

I laughed and punched him lightly on the arm.

"What?" he asked. "Beta's totally hot!"

I reached over and grabbed his hand. "I think you're pretty hot too."

When we got back to the cottage, the sun was beginning to set, and it had turned significantly cooler. "Wow, the temps really drop when the sun goes down, huh?"

"Yep, they can, but I'll get a fire going, and we can put this frozen pizza in the oven and snuggle by the fire while we eat it."

"I like the way you think, *Indigo* Freemont."

While the pizza was cooking, I slipped into the bathroom to take advantage of the huge, beautiful soaking tub I'd spied in the ensuite. I was happy to find some delicious bubble bath next to the tub, then let myself soak the long ride and busy afternoon away. When I got out, I put on my sexy lingerie I'd bought just for this occasion, under my jeans and T-shirt.

By the time we were snuggled in front of the fire, and the pizza was mostly eaten, I was happy and content as I snuggled with my man. He had fixed us each a glass of wine, and mine, along with the earlier bubble bath, had caused me to feel like soft putty.

"You look like you are about to fall asleep, Suzie," Indi said into my hair, before he kissed my head.

"I'm just content. You?" I asked.

"I'm content too." We lay back again, but then he said, "Suzie, let's go to bed and be content there."

I looked up at him, the excitement of what this could mean causing my heart to speed up.

"Shhh," he said. "Calm down. We don't have to do anything, but I want to snuggle with you and feel your skin against mine."

I only nodded, because I knew unless I totally freaked out, I would definitely be looking for more tonight than just cuddling.

I went into the bathroom to brush my teeth, and stared at myself in the mirror. "If I don't take this bull by the horns—or in this case horn—I'm never going to go all the way." I knew Indi would never push, and I knew if I let myself think, I'd freak out, so as I said to my reflection, "Okay, take the bull by the horn!"

I stripped down to the sexy bra and panties then pulled the matching see-through negligee over them. I came out of the bathroom, letting myself pause dramatically in the bathroom door, until Indi noticed me.

When he did, his eyes grew three times bigger in size, which made me chuckle. I could almost see the man salivating, and for the first time in my life, that didn't worry me in the least. In fact, I intended to take full advantage of it.

# Indi

When Suzie came out of the bathroom, I had expected her to be in her regular sleep clothes. I had no expectations, as I had explained to her before. She had to take the lead on this one, and until we got past this next sexual step, I knew I'd have to give her all the space she needed. The truth was that I was totally cool with that.

Sleeping with Suzie, and exploring her body in the ways she felt comfortable, was like striking gold. She was sensual and responsive. When my mouth covered her breasts, she would breathe in and make a little sexy sound as the intensity took hold of her.

I was imagining letting my tongue glide down her stomach to more interesting areas, when she walked out of the bathroom, and struck a pose in the doorway.

I thought my heart was going to fall out of my chest and do flip-flops on the floor. Suzie had changed into this sexy number, red with naughty black lace, that was covered with a negligee that was clearly only for show. But, oh my god, what a show! I'd swear, this made my dick stand at attention more than the Beta costume did.

When she saw my face, she smiled that sexy, naughty smile, and sauntered over to where I sat on the side of the bed.

I couldn't hold back my thoughts, "You are so beautiful, so..." I couldn't find the words to express how much she affected me.

Suzie didn't respond, but instead pushed me back onto the bed, and let her mouth take mine.

She devoured me, nipping at my bottom lip. She straddled me, and where the lace brushed up against my stomach, electricity shot through me. As she kissed my neck and then down to my nipples, she bit down, causing me to feel the sensation down to my already-throbbing cock.

She let her tongue glide along my stomach muscles as she unbuttoned my pants, pulling them down, so that I sprang out. Suzie rubbed her stomach over me, and I thought I was going to come then and there, before I'd even become fully exposed.

She crawled off me, and said, "Take them the rest of the way off."

I did as she said, then crawled back onto the bed on my knees, so I could embrace her, and take her mouth with mine.

She had other ideas, though, and pushed me back onto the bed. She let her tongue move back down my stomach, causing the muscles to contract with her touch. Once she found my cock again, she took me into her mouth. I moaned, but had to push her back. "Suzie, I'm too close. I'm going to come if you push anymore."

She just chuckled and went back to sucking me. As I predicted, I didn't last long—the woman had too much control over me. Suzie sat up and used her finger to wipe off her lips.

"My god, Suzie, *that* was hot!" She laughed, then she straddled me again, running her hands over my chest and torso. "You got anything else left in you?" she asked, with the mischievous grin on her lips again.

"Yep!" I said, and gently pushed her off of me. "Give me the reins for a moment?" I asked, and she looked skeptical. "Trust me?" I coaxed, and she nodded.

I used my tongue as I'd fantasized about before seeing her in the doorway, exploring all her sensitive areas while I let my hands explore her. When I removed her panties, I once again watched for any discomfort, but finding only desire, I continued until she was naked from the waist down.

I used my mouth and tongue to explore her. When she began to writhe with pleasure, I deepened and sped up my actions until she began to vibrate with need. I used my fingers to enhance the experience, and Suzie crested, bucking against my mouth.

I leaned up and smiled. The woman looked even more delicious with a satisfied look on her face. I swore to myself I would do whatever I had to do in the future to keep putting that look there.

I was about to go in for round two, when Suzie crawled over me and went over to the light switch and turned it off. The only light in the room now came from the bathroom. She seemed to know just where to stand so that the light illuminated her beautiful form. She took the negligee off and let it slip to the floor then moved closer to me as she unhooked her bra. She allowed it to slide delightfully slowly down her arms, then she placed the bra on the bedpost and crawled up next to me.

She looked down, and seeing that I was throbbing once again said, "I think it's ready for round two."

I gulped, completely taken by this incredible woman.

This time when Suzie straddled me, she moved her body right over my erection, until I thought I was going to burst again.

She began to rub up and down until I could feel her natural lubrication. She was filled with as much desire as I was, and she leaned over and kissed me.

I reached over to the bedstand, and retrieved the condom and lube I'd stashed there. "Give me a second," I said, and she rolled off of me as I put it on.

As soon as I was done, Suzie crawled back on top of me and began rubbing up and down me again. As she did, I penetrated her and she gasped. She bit down on my lower lip, and after the initial surprise subsided, she glided me inside her even further. She moaned as she bored down all the way, taking me completely, and riding the waves of our joined desire.

I watched her to see if she was still enjoying the sensation, and seeing no pain registered, I began to thrust. Quickly, she joined my rhythm, and I slowed down and sped up, according to how her body language dictated.

Suzie rode me, clearly in her own ecstasy. Seeing her taken by the sensation, caused me to soar as well, and I came, exploding into the condom.

When she crawled off of me, I removed the spent condom, wrapping it in a tissue next to the bed and tossed it toward a trash can that sat in the corner of the room. I leaned over her wanting to give *her* my full attention now.

I moved down and let my tongue explore her, wanting, no needing to see her crest again one more time. As I explored her, I could tell she was close as she began to moan, and arch beneath me. When she came, she did so calling my name, which caused my insides to react in all sorts of funny ways.

I all but fell on top of her, kissing her, and then I rolled over, letting myself enjoy the post-sexual bliss.

Before I could doze off, I asked, "Was that okay?"

She just nodded, then said, "That was so fucking awesome."

"Have you never come that often before?" I asked.

She shook her head.

"Not even when you did it to yourself?" I asked.

"No, not that many times."

"Wanna do it again?"

She smiled, "Oh yeah," and leaned over to kiss me again. As she did, she said under her breath, "Damn, it's good to be a woman."

"Yeah, you know, I'm gonna need a moment. But if you give me time, I promise to overcome my limitations."

We both laughed and fell asleep in each other's arms.

I woke up a couple hours later to go pee. When I came back, I snuggled close, rubbing her shoulders until she began to stir. "Can I do it again now?" I asked. The thought of making her come again as she woke up sent chills along my spine.

She nodded at me and grinned without opening her eyes. As I moved over her, she stretched and moaned until I succeeded with what I was hoping to accomplish. After I chased and found her second orgasm, she put her hands up saying, "Enough, I need to sleep."

I chuckled, and kissed her. "You tell me if or when you want me to resume. I'm at your beck and call, My Lady," I said. She chuckled too, and we fell back in bed, and back asleep in each other's arms.

I woke again as the sun was just coming up. This time Suzie was coming back from the bathroom. I teased her, saying she didn't get much sleep. She flopped into bed beside me, and said if she could do this every night, then she'd never have to sleep again.

I was afraid to do too much penetration on her first night. I figured we should explore other ways of allowing her to have as many fond memories of her first time as possible. What I didn't take into consideration was what Suzie wanted.

Suzie straddled me once again. I was erect, and she was about to ride me, when I said, "Wait, I need to grab a condom."

Suzie smiled down at me. "When was the last time you were tested?"

"Um, about six months ago, and I'm negative. But there are other things to worry about, like a baby!" I said, speaking the obvious.

Suzie chuckled. "I'm negative too, although it's a given, since I've never gone past second base with anyone, but I've been tested too. I'm also on birth control. So, we should be good."

I nodded, and when she began to rock back and forth on me again, I was in no frame of mind to argue with her.

As she rode me, her hair fell down in front of her. I moaned and grabbed her hips, moving my body in rhythm to hers.

"I never knew this could feel so good," she said. "I always thought it would hurt, but it just feels *so damned good*."

All I could do at that point was to ride the wave and enjoy the pleasure we were both experiencing.

As she moved, she became increasingly more aggressive, heightening my pleasure.

"Oh, god, Suzie! I'm going to come. My god, you need to stop now," I said, but she was too far gone to pull back.

After my orgasm, she fell off of me and landed at my side, so she was lying half on top of me.

Within moments, Suzie's stomach began to growl.

"Um, I think that thing is hungry," I said.

"That thing, is it?" she said, teasing me back.

"Yeah, your stomach is a miracle. It can hold immense amounts of food."

"I'm an athlete," she said. "You try dancing around a mega stage while singing and see if you don't get hungry."

"Honey, I wasn't complaining, just admiring another amazing part of your anatomy."

Suzie crawled out of bed, slipped into the shower, and before I knew it, she was singing. If I remembered correctly, it was the song she sang in the musical after Beta first fell in love with Lydia.

*My Dearest*, I thought as I listened to her sing, *if that is any indication how you feel, I'm right there with you.*

# Suzie

I came out of the shower, and the bed was made. I slipped on my bathrobe, and went into the kitchen to find Indi cooking breakfast. I could smell the bacon frying, and my mouth immediately began watering.

"I love bacon," I moaned, and Indi turned around with a mischievous grin.

"I've been hearing that moan all night, and now, after all that work, I find out all I needed to do was cook bacon?"

I laughed, and came over to put my arms around his waist.

"I like bacon, but I like your tongue more," she said.

Indi chuckled, low and sensual, and said, "Your tongue was pretty amazing itself."

# Indi

As we drove back toward New York, neither of us was keen on ending the weekend, but I had to be back to work Tuesday morning. As it was, I was taking my life in my hands for taking Monday morning off.

"What's your plans next weekend?" I asked.

"Back on the regular schedule, so I'm free Sunday and Monday." She looked at me expectantly.

"As you know, my friends have asked me to be their baby's godfather. They're having a gender reveal in a couple months. Would you consider coming with me?"

Suzie looked at me with appraising eyes. "Of course, I'll come with you if you want me to. Where is it?"

"New Haven," I replied. "So, it'll be another long drive I'm afraid."

Suzie thought for a moment and when I gave her the date for the event, she quickly asked "How about we take a plane?"

"We could, but after you go through security and all the insanity, it takes longer than just driving."

Suzie just smiled at me. "Are you afraid of heights?"

I glanced at her to see where this was headed. "I'm not especially afraid of heights, no, but..."

"Well, then, my friend Jake owns his own plane. He's been trying to get me to take a flight with him, but I haven't had the time, or rather, didn't want to take the time. I know he flies up to New Haven. If we went with him, it could cut at least an hour off the trip, maybe two."

I sat staring out at the road, trying not to let the jealousy slip in, but I was having no luck. Suzie finally picked up on it, and said, "Remember, all my guy friends are gay, so I'm not going to be the person he is checking out on the flight."

I laughed out loud, glanced back at her, and said, "Am I that transparent?"

"Oh, yeah, you had already taken on the same green as the Grinch."

"Humph. Well, I just got you, so I sure as hell don't want to share you."

"Not even with a gay guy?" She was still teasing me.

"Gay guys don't bother me at all," I replied. "It's good for you to have girlfriends." I chuckled.

"So, what are your thoughts about the flying?" she asked again.

"I don't know, to be honest. I've never flown in anything smaller than a jet."

"Don't worry, Honey, I'll be right there with you."

Something about the way she was smiling had all my self-preservation instincts humming.

"I'll text him and find out if he's available that weekend."

Within a few minutes, it was confirmed. *What the hell have I gotten myself into?*

***

The eight weeks since we'd spent the weekend in the Hamptons had flown by. Suzie usually wasn't available through the week, but we snuck in a night or two when we could. I'd either meet her at her apartment with food and wine, and we'd make love, or she'd drag me out to the bar and/or Vinnie's Diner.

My favorite times, though, were Sunday and Monday, when we had time to just snuggle in and enjoy being together.

We met Suzie's friend, Jake, at the airport, and climbed aboard. The guy was tall, rugged, and handsome, and if I hadn't known he was gay, I was sure I'd have felt insecure. I really did need to work on whatever was making me the jealous type all of a sudden.

After the plane was airborne, I was intent on thinking about our happy times together as the plane hit turbulence for what had to be the hundredth time. I gave Suzie an expression which must have been a mixture between anger and fear for my life. What in the hell was I thinking, flying to New Haven in a tuna-fish can?

Her friend Jake was enjoying my misery as much as Suzie. The plane bumped through the sky, and I thanked god that I hadn't eaten breakfast that morning.

When we landed, I jumped down the stairs as quickly as I could. It took all my willpower not to fall and kiss the ground. Suzie and Jake laughed at me as they walked past and into the hangar that attached to his family home.

When I regained enough composure, I stared, shocked, at the mega mansion in front of me.

"Jake, are you some kind of mobster or something?" I said, as I took in my surroundings.

Jake just chuckled, and said, "Or something…"

"Jake's parents own several hotels in New England," Suzie said, then smiled like she'd just told me Jake liked wearing jeans.

It was still early when we arrived. Jake invited us in for breakfast, which was served by his staff. Then, we took our leave, but not before he reminded us that he needed to head out Monday before five to get back to New York. I was determined to figure out a way to get back home without flying in that death trap, but figured it wasn't the right time to bring that up.

I'd rented a car, and it had been delivered to Jake's address, which Suzie had given me when I was making plans. We left Jake's and headed to Dalton and Kristina's place.

Dalton and Kristina both took to Suzie from the moment they met. Kristina had seen *Gerls* on Broadway when she was in New York for a girls' weekend. I had told them that Suzie was on Broadway, and Kristina had figured it out from her name, which show she was in.

Luckily, after the first few minutes of Kristina singing the praises of the show, Suzie was allowed to just be one of us, and the star-struck part of the night was over.

We ordered our normal pizza, which Suzie ate most of. When Dalton and I went out to the garage, Suzie and Kristina stayed back. It was almost like we'd been doing this all our lives.

When we came back in, Kristina was sitting across from Suzie, and they were talking like old friends. Occasionally, Kristina would say something to Suzie that would cause her to belt out a laugh. When they both looked at me, I had a feeling they were discussing me.

"Dalton. Dude," I said over my shoulder when he walked in behind me, "I kind of get the feeling I've walked into the lion's den."

Dalton laughed. "Oh, man, you have no idea. And here is a bit of advice from someone who has had to learn to live with my wife and her women friends—ignore what you can, and what you can't—just smile and try to look innocent!"

I nodded, and Dalton walked with me past the women, and into the kitchen.

"So, what are the plans?" I asked him.

"Well, it's a shower, and normally, we'd be able to escape and run to the pub down the street, but I've been informed that the 1950s are over, so I'm obligated to be there, which means, you are obligated to be there as well."

"Any idea what this whole thing will consist of?"

"The easy answer is no. I've been told something about lots of games, and some sexy jokes, but no specifics have been shared."

"I get the feeling this is going to be torture," I responded.

Dalton just nodded, a gleam coming to his eyes. "That is the main reason I asked you to be the kid's godfather. Now, you'll have to endure this kind of stuff with me."

There wasn't much I could do, other than shake my head and give Dalton a nasty look, as if to say, *Payback is hell, Dude, hell!*

***

Kristina's parents had already arrived shortly after we'd got settled in. Suzie had gone upstairs for a nap, and when she came down, Kristina's mom, Patty, was cooking at the stove. She literally screamed when she saw Suzie. Apparently, she had been on the girls' weekend when they had all gone to Suzie's show.

Luckily, just like with Kristina, Patty and Suzie hit it off, and within moments, all three women were bunched around the kitchen island, chatting.

"Can I help with anything?" I asked.

"No," Patty said. "I don't like a lot of cooks in the kitchen. Why don't you join Dalton and Pete in the living room? I think they're about to declare war on one another."

I walked into the living room, leaving the women, and found the other two men debating which game they were going to play. Dalton and his father-in-law had been fierce rivals ever since Dalton once said that no one in his father-in-law's generation could ever beat someone his age at a video game. Every time I'd come to visit Dalton when his father-in-law was there, they would be head-to-head in some game. In fact, Pete actually won as often as Dalton did.

Lunch was served with lots of conversation and laughter. The few times I'd met Kristina's family, I'd really enjoyed them. Just as they had embraced me, they embraced Suzie as well.

Friends and family soon began to arrive, and it was quickly apparent that Dalton's family was the polar opposite of Kristina's.

Dalton's parents were very involved in politics, and therefore were always trying to keep up appearances. Dalton confided early on how different he was from them. He never invited me to be around them, although they had told him that they liked that

Dalton hung out with me, since I came from such a distinguished family. I understood what they were implying. My family had been quite wealthy before my parents had spent most of the money on trivial things. The Freemont name still held some sway in the upper circles of New York. It probably also helped that my parents still contributed handsomely to the same brand of politics that Dalton's parents did.

Dalton, Pete, and I were on kitchen duty, while Suzie, Kristina, and Patty all set to work prepping the living room for the shower. We were all finishing up our assigned duties, when Dalton's parents showed up at the door. When they were introduced to Suzie, the chill factor raised significantly, causing Suzie to glance at me with a questioning look.

I tried to be as friendly as possible as I excused Suzie and myself, to go upstairs to clean up for the party. I explained Dalton's parents to her, and she nodded.

"I see," she said. "I doubt the very conservative would be fond of my show, and definitely would not be too fond of my part, huh?"

"No, I doubt they would be," I replied.

"Well, I'll be on my best behavior," she said. "But, I warn you, I won't try to change who I am, just because someone disapproves of me."

I went over and pulled Suzie into a hug. "My Dearest, I would hate to see you try to change anything about the incredible woman I've become so fond of."

Suzie smiled, then kissed me.

"I'm pretty fond of you too, Indi," she said, and we finished getting ready.

By the time we got downstairs, there was a crew of Kristina's friends at work decorating the first floor. Suzie was immediately pulled into the fray as she was fawned over as a star, but more importantly another set of decorating hands.

The shower started around five, and tons of guests poured through the door. Dalton's parents had set up their own area in the den behind the kitchen. Kristina's parents were in the living room and dining room. There was a definite distinction between the two parties. Dalton tended to stay in between. I told Suzie to go join the fun party and I'd hang with Dalton to keep him company as he endeavored to mitigate the two different groups of people.

Around five thirty, according to Kristina, all the guests had arrived, and therefore, we should eat. Dalton's parents had hired a caterer, so mounds of food lay in the kitchen. Most if it was posh finger food, and when Suzie came to check on me, I whispered in her ear that we'd go eat real food later.

She was laughing when the front door opened, and in walked a man dressed in a three-piece suit, and a woman who should've been attractive, except that her face was pinched in what appeared to be a perpetual frown.

I felt Suzie stiffen beside me, and when I looked down at her, I saw that she had gone pale.

I started to ask her what was wrong, when Dalton's mother dashed past us, almost knocking us over to get to the couple.

"Oh, you made it," his mother exclaimed.

Then, she turned to the entire room. Raising her voice so that everyone could hear her, she announced to the party that the soon-to-be Connecticut Senator had arrived. She even asked that everyone give him a round of applause.

Most of the Kristina's guests tentatively clapped while the group who'd been in the back room with Dalton's parents hooted and yelled. It was a strange dynamic that would've amused me, if Suzie hadn't begun gripping my hand.

Then, as if in a horror film, the man turned and looked Suzie in the eye. A nasty grin spread across his face. Before he turned away, he made a production of looking down her body and back up to her face. The way he licked his lips made me uncomfortable, so I could imagine what it'd done to Suzie.

The man turned to Mrs. Malloy and thanked her, then, as if he were standing in front of a political rally, he spoke for over fifteen minutes to the group about the need to undo the establishment that had led to the demise of family values. Although he never said anything directly, he indirectly insulted almost every culture and belief system different from his own.

Kristina stood across the room, her face a bright red, and Dalton's head was bowed through most of the speech.

When the idiot finally stopped talking, Dalton's parents and their small band clapped loudly, while the rest of the group stared at one another. A few clapped, more to alleviate the awkward feeling in the room, than in appreciation of what he'd said.

Finally, Patty stood up, and said, "Thank you, sir, for the, ummm... speech. Now back to eating. Everyone grab a plate."

Suzie hadn't moved since the politician came into the room—at least not until he began walking toward her.

"Well, if it isn't my old *friend*, Suzie Fisher," he said with a distinct slur, letting his eyes travel down her body again, almost like he owned her. It took everything in me not to go male postal on him, but being a possessive silverback ape wouldn't do anyone any good.

Suzie seemed to regain some of her posture and responded, "What makes you think we're friends, *Eddie?*"

The man just smiled and said, "People call me Edward these days." Then, he examined Suzie in a snobby way, and added, "At least the people who matter."

Suzie stiffened again, but let her voice drop to a whisper, quiet enough that only Edward and I could hear. "Edward, do the people who *matter* know you attempted to rape me?"

All the humor dropped from the man's face, and I could tell he had to restrain himself. "Your lies don't matter here," he said before he walked away.

When he left, I gave Suzie a questioning look. She just shook her head, and then turned toward the door. I followed her as she walked out of the house, and headed down the street.

"Suzie," I said as I followed behind her. "What's going on? Who is that man?"

Suzie just shook her head and kept walking. We went several blocks before she finally stopped, and sat on a bench that faced the bay.

I came over and sat next to her. I hadn't known Suzie for long, but I'd known her long enough to know when she was really upset, and I knew that idiot of a politician had done something to both intimidate and enrage her. I didn't want to rush her, so I sat quietly until she spoke.

"That man..." she said, then hesitated. She looked over at me and said, "Do you remember when I told you something happened to me in high school?" I nodded. "I was headed to my prom, when the guy I was with, pulled over and tried to rape me. Luckily, the dress I had on was too much, but the boy did pull his dick out, and started masturbating on me." She leaned back and closed her eyes. "What a fucking mess," she said.

"Suzie," I said, since she had clearly gone into her head.

She opened her eyes, and looked directly at me. "That son of a bitch who came in, that was him. Eddie Fucking McPeak." That was when the tears began to flow.

I pulled her into my arms, and she snuggled closer.

"I'm so sorry, Suzie," I said, trying to comfort her.

"How the hell did he end up here, and running for senator in Connecticut?" I asked.

Suzie just shrugged, and cried some more. "I can't go back and face him right now," she said. "I know that makes me weak, but..."

I cut her off. "It doesn't make you weak, Suzie. Don't say that. Have you seen him since you were a kid?"

She shook her head. "He moved right after that. I never knew where he went."

I nodded with understanding. "Well, fuck. What do you want to do?" I asked.

Suzie just shook her head again, while she continued to lean into me.

Finally, she wiped her eyes. "Why don't we go get another pizza," she said. "No offense to Kristina, but that food looked plastic."

I smiled, but I knew Suzie was trying to lift the mood. "It was pretty awful looking," I agreed. "The pizza place is about another half mile from here. Should I go back and get the rental car?"

"No, it was blocked in by other guests. Let's just walk there," she said.

Suzie was quiet most of the way. I didn't try to force the conversation, guessing she had a lot on her mind. When we got to the restaurant, she told me to order what I wanted, while she called her parents. She'd be back in a moment. I agreed and she went to sit on a bench beside the restaurant, and got out her phone.

# Suzie

When Mom answered my phone call, all I could do was cry. Luckily, she instinctively knew it was me, and didn't hang up. I cried in her ear for what seemed like fifteen minutes, before I could find my voice.

"He's here," I finally told her. "He's here in Connecticut, running for the fucking Senate."

My mother was fast, and didn't need to ask who I was talking about. "Fuck," was all she said as I continued to weep into her ear.

"Want me to come kill him?" This time it was my father's voice.

The abruptness of his comment made me laugh. "No, Dad, not really, but I might fantasize about that a little over the next few days if you don't mind."

"Then, that'll be both of us fantasizing about it, Sweetheart," he said.

"Where are you, Honey?" Mom asked.

"I'm at a party with Indi, the man I told you I started seeing. His best friend is having a shower. The friend's parents invited the asshole to the party. He just came in like he owned the damned place." I was trying not to shake so much that I would drop the phone.

"Where is Indi right now?" Mom asked.

"He's in a pizza place we walked to. He's ordering pizza for us."

"Can I talk to him?"

"Mom, that might not be a good idea. What are you going to say to him? This isn't his fault."

"Honey, I wasn't going to blame him, I was going to give him our information, so he could reach us if you needed us."

"Mom, I'm fine. It was just a shock to my system. I haven't seen him all this time, and then he just showed up in my face."

"Okay, Baby, but you give Indi our number anyway. Will you promise that?"

"Yeah, Mom, I will."

"Do you want us to fly up there?" Dad asked.

At this point, I just laughed. I knew my parents had my back, and that's what I needed to be reminded of.

"You're the best parents in the world, do you both know that?"

"Of course we do, Honey," Dad said.

"No, I don't need you to fly up here, but thanks for your willingness to."

"You only have to ask, and we'll be on the next flight."

"I know, Mom."

"Reconsider me hiring a hit man too. Okay, Hon?" my father said—not in a joking way.

"I'm not going to need you to kill him, Dad, but thanks for asking that, too. Okay, I'm going to go into the pizza place, have too much pizza to eat, and cuddle with my boyfriend. Then, I'm going to call my friend, and fly back to the city. Thanks, you guys, for having my back. I love you."

"We love you too," my parents both replied at the same time.

I hung up and took a moment to collect myself, before going back into the restaurant. The last thing I needed was some amateur to take a picture with their mobile phone of me crying like a lunatic in public. I could just see the press making up some ridiculous story to go with that picture.

I went back into the restaurant and directly into the bathroom and washed my face. Yeah, my makeup had taken a beating, but it was better than it was with black streaks running down my face. Damn, I loved my job, but sometimes I hated that I had to be presentable one hundred percent of the time.

Luckily, I came out of the bathroom just as Indi was picking up the box of pizza.

He gestured toward the door, and I followed him out and toward a little park with a couple picnic tables looking out over the bay.

When we sat down, Indi looked at me for a moment, and asked, "Are you okay here, or do you want me to call a taxi to take us somewhere less public?"

I smiled. This man was such a good one. Most guys wouldn't even consider my career or need for privacy. I looked around, and seeing that hardly anyone was out on the beach, and no one had seemed to recognize me, I figured we were okay.

"I'm good, Indi. Let's just eat the pizza and give me a little time to compose myself."

Indi nodded and opened the box. He handed me a plate and leaned over to kiss my forehead. "I'm sorry, Suzie. I wish I could go back and undo this afternoon."

"I guess I had to face him eventually. This is just my time," I replied, sighing. "Seriously, I don't want to think about him anymore. I want to stuff my face, and then I want to go get ice cream. We can go to the gym to work it all off later, okay?"

Indi nodded, but the look of concern didn't leave his face.

I never understood how incredible it felt to have strong arms around you when things were tough. Indi was more than a gentleman. If there could be two men more opposite than Eddie and Indi, I couldn't imagine who it was.

After we finished our pizza, Indi disposed of the boxes and plates, and then he walked with me cuddled next to him along the beach toward a place he said he knew there was ice cream. We walked like that for what had to be a couple miles, meandering along the seafront, in and out of shops. I'd forgotten where we were going by the time we made it to the ice-cream place. This was a good indication of how bad things were, because I never forgot ice cream.

I'd lost my appetite, though, so Indi ordered a sundae and sat next to me with two spoons. "Have a few bites," he said. "There's nothing like dairy and sugar to make the bad feel a little better."

I chuckled, having said the same thing more than a few times myself. I took a few bites, but it tasted bitter and caused my stomach to stir a bit. What I really wanted was to snuggle into Indi, and not think at all for a while.

When we got done, it was getting late. Indi called Dalton, who told him the party was over, and all the guests, including his parents, had left. He then got a taxi that took us back to their house.

I went straight up to the bedroom without talking to anyone. I felt bad about it, but I couldn't face anyone just yet, and I sure didn't want to explain why I was so upset.

Luckily, when I got in touch with Jake, he said he was happy to leave the next morning if I was ready to go.

Indi agreed with the early departure, and let his friends know we were going to leave early. We headed out before the sun rose the next morning. Kristina was awake as we were leaving. She had two coffees in to-go cups ready to hand to us as we walked out the door.

Before we left, she pulled me into a hug, and said, "I don't know what that bastard did, or why you were upset, but I promise to God, he will never set foot in this house again. You, on the other hand, are always welcome here, do you understand?"

The tears spilled out of my eyes, before I could stop them, and Kristina pulled me back into a hug.

The flight back to New York was smooth—a lot smoother than the flight to get there. I was glad about that, because I knew Indi was dreading it, and because I didn't have the strength to comfort him if he needed it.

When we got back, I hugged Jake and thanked him for letting us fly with him to Connecticut.

Indi and I didn't speak much as we rode in the taxi back to my apartment. He seemed to sense that I needed to be by myself, so he dropped me off without offering to come up. Indi got out of the taxi, took my bags out of the back and held me for several minutes.

"Call me when you're ready, okay?" he said.

I just nodded, got my bags, and headed up to the apartment.

When I was finally back in my own space, I collapsed on the bed, and let the tears I'd been holding back flow. I had no idea how long I cried before I fell asleep, but I didn't wake up until the next morning.

All the shock was gone, and in its place was the rage I'd held onto for so many years. That motherfucker had the audacity to come at *me*. That might just have been his last mistake, because this bitch had had enough!

Instead of going to the gym, I called my friend BJ, who owned a kickboxing studio. They were usually only open in the evenings, but when I told her I needed to work out some anger over a son of a bitch rapist, she said she'd meet me at the studio door.

I spent over an hour punching, kicking and working out the anger. When I was done, I was still pissed, but I was also comfortably tired. BJ told me I could come by anytime I needed to. I thanked her over and over, saying it was exactly what I needed. Then, I thanked her again for not asking questions.

"If you need a therapist, I'm not qualified, but if you need a place to metaphorically beat up a man, well... I've got you covered."

I chuckled at the quintessential BJness of that statement. She didn't cringe when I hugged her, despite being sweaty.

As I walked out, she said, "Seriously, you call if you need another session, okay?"

On the walk home, I felt my energy returning to normal. I was a powerful woman, strong and sure of myself. I was no longer the teenage girl who was defenseless. I had almost convinced myself of this, when I got to my complex door.

As I walked up the stairs, I was met by a man in his mid-thirties who was wearing a suit.

"Are you Miss Suzie Fisher?" he asked.

I nodded, unsure of what he was doing there, or why he was asking for me.

The man then reached into his briefcase, pulled out a bunch of papers and handed them to me. "Miss

Fisher, you've hereby been served." He walked off my stoop, got into a waiting vehicle and drove off.

I stared at the car, then looked at the envelope in my hand. When I opened it and pulled out papers, I immediately saw that I was being sued by Edward H. McPeak and that he'd gotten a temporary restraining and gag order against me. "What the fuck?"

***

After being served, I stared at my wall for quite a long while. I had to push this out of my head, and return to the show, but the next day I called both my parents and brother. Even after speaking to them, the shock still hadn't worn off. My parents encouraged me to contact my agent, who referred me to Howard Edgerton's law firm. He was well known in the New York theatrical circles, and she thought he'd be my best contact.

Then, she promptly fired me as her client. Evidently, she was a big advocate of Edward McPeak, and even worked on his campaign when she went home on the weekends.

If I were honest, I'd never liked my agent. We'd never shared the same personal views, but she was a bulldog in the industry. When I was new to the theater, my director had referred me to her, and she'd done a good job.

I would've fired her the day I found out that Indi was in the business, especially when I learned about his values. Unfortunately, he was pretty clear that we shouldn't combine personal business with professional. That would need to change now, because he was the only agent I had any interest in working with.

Mr. Edgerton interviewed me immediately, then advised that I stay away from Indi until a deposition could be held. He was the only person at the party, who could've heard what I said to Eddie, and therefore, he was essential to the case.

Eddie was alleging that I announced to the party that he had raped me, which would've served him right, but that wasn't what happened. Edgerton believed this was his attempt to silence me as quickly as possible. His words were, "After the Kavanaugh fiasco, the Conservative Party wouldn't be taking any chances in the future."

I shuddered at the way that sounded. I thought Edgerton was going to be a good attorney, and I certainly believed he had my best interests at heart, but I wondered if he had any idea what that whole "fiasco" had done to Dr. Blasey-Ford. No, he was a man. He wouldn't have understood it. In his mind, it was just chaos that needed to be managed. Hell, he probably thought the same about me.

He asked me upfront if I were willing to settle this out of court, by ensuring that I would remain silent. I immediately said no that I wouldn't be shut up by that man ever again.

"I would be remiss if I didn't warn you, Ms. Fisher, if this gets out, and it very well could get out, it may have a negative impact on your career." Then, he suggested that I speak to my agent. When I told him my boyfriend was going to be my new agent, he had the decency to hide his emotions.

"We will expedite the deposition, so you can speak with him, but we also have to be careful not to let the opposition know we're too eager. Otherwise, they will likely try to impede us."

In the end, they agreed to expedite the case as much as possible, because both of us were public figures, and it was just a matter of time before the press got word of the situation.

# Indi

After we got back from Connecticut, everything was quiet on the Suzie front. I had decided not to call her, knowing she would need her space. Rather, I would send an occasional text, reminding her that I cared about her, and that I was there for her if she needed me.

Besides the one- or two-word reply, I hadn't really heard back. Finally, I decided to sic my brother on her. Well, more precisely, Clay. If anyone could break through Suzie's darkness, it would be him.

I didn't want to share too much of Suzie's business, but one night when Denim and Clay were snuggling on the couch, I went down and asked them for a few minutes.

"Hey, I don't know if you've seen Suzie lately, but I know she's dealing with some shit, and it requires...

um... well, you know, someone who isn't sleeping with her to talk it out. Do you know what I mean?" I asked.

Clay didn't miss a beat. "You mean she needs her girlfriends," he said, waving his finger between himself and Denim.

"Well, yeah, I guess. She needs her friends. Can you two check up on her, and let me know if I need to do anything?"

Denim and Clay looked at each other, and smiles crossed their faces. "I think my brother has fallen in love," Denim said, teasing.

I stood up to leave, knowing this was all going to go south from here. "Just let me know if she needs me," I said as I walked away.

Clay and Denim began sing-songing, "Indi loves Suzie, Indi loves Suzie."

I just shook my head. They were total shits, but I knew they wouldn't ignore my request. Suzie needed friends right now, and no doubt Clay and Denim would be there for her.

# Suzie

Life got tough. I couldn't have contact with Indi. Clay and Denim tried to be supportive, but since they were close to Indi, I couldn't really involve them, so if it hadn't been for my brother, Aiden, I think I might've crashed and burned.

Aiden flew in from Washington, and stayed with me for about a week while all the crap was going on around me.

It wasn't like I was much fun, though. I cried most of the time, and I apologized for being such a dud.

"Suzie, you've got to stop apologizing," Aiden said. "I know things are hard. That's why I'm here."

This, of course, just made me cry more.

Finally, he started dragging *me* to the club, and would dance the intensity out of me. This probably helped more than anything. Falling back into the routine we had before he'd gone off and gotten married, was almost like things hadn't changed.

After Aiden left, my parents showed up. I was so lucky that I had a family that loved me, and even though we were all spread across the country, I could still depend on them to step in when things got ugly.

Indi showed up while my parents were still in town. I was just getting off stage and was about to head home, when I saw him.

I was devastated by how sad he looked, and I completely understood why. I felt the same way. We'd been together for such a short time, but he was still all I could think about.

It broke something inside me sending him away, but the attorney had been clear. I couldn't have contact with him, until a deposition was completed. Indi was my only proof I hadn't slandered the idiot, and that proof had to be irrefutable.

By the time my parents left, I was so desperate to have Indi back in my arms, it literally felt like a real physical ailment.

# Indi

As the days passed, I became increasingly more concerned about Suzie. Even the few texts I had gotten after we returned from Connecticut had dried up. Occasionally, I would get a thumbs up when I texted her, but more often than not, she just ignored me completely.

Not for the first time, I had a strong desire to do damage to that politician's face. He had done such a number on Suzie, and now she was distancing herself from me. No way was I going to be able to allow that to go on for long.

When I questioned Clay and Denim, they hedged. They assured me she was okay, but they wouldn't elaborate on the details.

"Is she breaking up with me?" I asked.

Both Clay and Denim quickly assured me that wasn't the case, but that Suzie had some issues, that included me, that she needed to work out. That was all they'd tell me.

I knew Suzie had time off coming up, so on her last night before the break, I showed up at her dressing room. She came in with a burst of energy, which seemed to evaporate the moment she saw me.

The look on her face said all I needed to know. She was full out dreading me. Despite the heartache, I understood there was nothing to be done, other than leave and give her space.

As I stood to go, Suzie came over. She looked me in the eye then pulled me into a hug. When the other cast members turned to leave, Suzie stopped them, saying, "I may need you to be my witnesses, so please stay."

"Indi, I'm sorry. I miss you terribly, but I can't speak to you, at least not right now. I'm not avoiding you, but my attorney said I can't talk to you until... well, until later." A tear slipped down her cheek.

"Wha–what?" I stammered. "Attorney?"

Suzie nodded. "I'm being sued, Indi, and you're my only witness, so my attorney said I couldn't talk to you. In fact, I shouldn't have even told you that much.

He should be calling you Monday with the details. I'm sorry, Indi. I miss you so much."

With that, Suzie sniffed, hugged me again, then walked out of the dressing room.

The other performers had witnessed this divide between Suzie and me. Several followed her, but the ones who stayed behind tried to comfort me. One even said, "She really cares a lot about you. She tells us all the time."

I couldn't do much other than nod.

When I left, I didn't know what to do. I'm not an aggressive man, but I totally wanted to hit something—or actually, someone. Instead, I went to the gym and tried to work out my frustrations. It didn't work, and I ended up going home and staring at the ceiling most of the night. I had figured out the person suing her was the prick from Connecticut. Why he was suing her, I didn't know. One thing was for sure. I would find a way to destroy that man if he hurt her or her career. That was a promise I made to her, and to myself!

***

Monday afternoon, I got a call I didn't recognize on my mobile. I usually ignored those phone calls, because they tended to be bogus, spam calls, but because Suzie told me to expect the attorney, I answered.

"Mr. Freemont?" the voice asked.

"Yes, this is him," I replied.

"Hello, this is Clayton Evans with the Times. We have information that your girlfriend Suzie Fisher has been served with a temporary restraining order from Edward McPeak. Would you be willing to give us a comment on that subject?"

*Damn!* I thought to myself. I'd dealt with the press as an agent before, and I'd always told my clients to tell friends and family never to talk to them without someone supervising the discussion.

I clicked off the phone without answering, and immediately texted Suzie.

*"Suzie, I know you told me not to contact you until I speak with your attorney, but I just got contacted by the press. They know about the TRO."*

Suzie texted me back immediately. *"I'll have my attorney call you now."*

It took less than thirty minutes for me to receive the call. Of course, not wanting to take another chance, I let the call go to voicemail, then when I got the message, I called the attorney back. He told me a little about the situation, and asked if I could come in that day for an interview.

I said I could, and had my assistant reschedule my afternoon meetings.

When I arrived at the attorney's office, I was escorted into a large conference room. Shortly after I arrived, a portly, middle-aged man came in carrying a handful of papers.

"Hello, Mr. Freemont, I'm Howard Edgerton, and I'm Suzie Fisher's counsel. I'm sorry to have you come in on such short notice, but this is rather urgent, especially if the press is now involved."

"It was my pleasure, sir, but I admit, I have no idea what this is about. I haven't spoken to Suzie other than at her dressing room in a crowd of actors and a few cryptic texts since we returned from our trip to Connecticut."

"That's good, that's good," the portly man said absentmindedly. "It's best if you haven't been together, at least until the deposition."

"Mr. Freemont, your girlfriend is being sued for slander by Mr. Edward H. McPeak. Miss Fisher said you were privy to the conversation between her and Mr. McPeak at a baby shower and gender reveal party in Connecticut. Is that correct?"

I nodded.

"Oh, I'm sorry, son, I'm recording this conversation. I should've told you that. Let's start again. "Do you mind if I record this conversation?"

"No, I don't mind." I said.

"Good, good. This case has the potential to be rather explosive, so I want to make sure I don't accidentally give the other side any ammunition. I'll ask you again, were you present at the time when Mr. McPeak and Miss Fisher met at your friend's house in Connecticut?"

I nodded, then remembered I was being recorded. "Yes, I was there."

The attorney nodded. "Did you hear the entire conversation?"

"Yes, I did," I confirmed.

"Did Miss Fisher speak to Mr. McPeak any time when you were *not* present?"

"No, she was with me the entire time."

"Good, good, that's what I needed to know. You confirmed what she'd told me herself. Now, Mr. Freemont, I need to ask you what you heard. Please be very specific about what both of them said. If you can't remember, you can just tell me, 'I don't remember,' okay?"

I nodded then said, "Okay."

I thought back over the events of that day, trying to remember all the details. "Suzie was standing next to me, when the guy showed up. I immediately noticed something was off, because Suzie stiffened beside me. When I looked down at her, she had gone pale."

"Did he come over to speak to her then?" the attorney asked.

"No," I replied. "He recognized her immediately, though, but he turned to the crowd, and made some ridiculous speech about a bunch of garbage. I honestly don't remember anything he said, but it was mostly bogus, I remember thinking that."

"That's okay. Do you remember what happened after the man gave his speech?"

"Yes, he shook hands with some people, then came over to where Suzie and I were standing."

"Do you remember what he said to her?"

"Not exactly, but when Suzie called him Eddie, he told her people called him Edward, or at least people who mattered called him Edward."

The attorney nodded. "I need you to be very specific now. Do you remember exactly what Suzie said in reply?"

I nodded, then quickly said yes, again, forgetting I was being recorded. "Yeah, I remember exactly what she said, because it shocked me. She said, 'Do the people who matter know you tried to rape me?'"

"And you are one-hundred-percent sure that's what she said?" he asked me, leaning in, and looking me dead in the eye.

"Yeah, I'm pretty close to one-hundred-percent sure that's what she said."

The attorney leaned back in his chair then, and said, "I've contacted Mr. McPeak's attorney, and have asked him to give me times for your deposition. The testimony you just gave me is paramount to this case. During the deposition, do you think you would say the same thing you have to me?"

"Yeah... Yes, of course," I replied. "Why wouldn't it be the same?"

The old man just smiled. "No reason."

Then his smile faded. "I need to ask that you not contact Suzie until after the deposition. We want to preserve your testimony, and I'm afraid if you speak with Suzie, it will take some of the credibility out of what you are saying. Do you agree?"

I sat for a moment. I was not happy about being separated from Suzie, but having worked with legal issues through the agency, I knew the attorney was a person's best chance of making it through a tough situation.

"I'll agree, but you better make that deposition as soon as you can. Suzie must be going through hell right now, and she needs all the support she can get."

The old man nodded sagely. "I agree, but she also needs a good defense. I'll speed up the process as much as I can. You have a good day, Mr. Freemont." Then he stood and left the room.

The entire session had been bizarre. I left and went back to work, bewildered and confused.

Just before I went home for the day, I got a call on my office line from Mr. Edgerton's office. The deposition could be held on the following Monday if I was available. Luckily, I had a pretty clean schedule that day, so I agreed. I only had seven days to wait, then I'd be able to reconnect with Suzie. I would do what she needed me to do, but damn if I didn't miss her.

***

The deposition was intense, but fast. Mr. Edgerton introduced McPeak's attorney. Luckily, the asshole didn't show up, although I had been warned by friends to expect him. The deposition went a lot easier, I thought, since he didn't.

Suzie was in the office, but she wasn't part of the deposition. That too was better, I thought, because I missed her enough that I thought I'd be distracted if she were there.

Mr. Edgerton asked basically the same questions he had asked the week before. I answered them pretty much the same way, and I felt confident when the old man smiled after he was done questioning me.

McPeak's attorney acted bored, a strategy I assumed he'd practiced. Unfortunately for him, I spent my life working with actors and actresses, and he would never have the skills those people had. So, I did to him what I did to them—I ignored his actions and tried to focus on his words.

"Do you have a sexual relationship with Miss Fisher?" he asked.

"That is none of your business," I replied, matter of fact.

"Well, if you are lying for her, then yes, it is," the man replied.

I just stared at him. I had seen these tactics before with some of my clients. Unhinge with accusations, then go in for the kill. I learned long ago, it was best to remain quiet, and let them trip over their own game.

We stared at each other for several moments, before he went on, "Are you certain Miss Fisher said the exact words you stated earlier?"

"Yes," I replied.

"What if there are others who are testifying, they heard Miss Fisher say something different?"

"They would be lying," I said, trying to keep my answers matter-of-fact.

"And so you are the only one who isn't lying?" the man asked, incredulous.

"I'm the only one who heard what was said, so yes, anyone else would be lying."

I noticed Suzie's attorney wince a bit at that, and I realized I'd let too much information go.

"You were the only one at the party?" the attorney asked.

I decided to go back to my one syllable answers if possible.

"No," I replied.

"You just said you were the only one who heard Suzie and Mr. McPeak speaking. Isn't that correct?"

"Yes," I agreed.

"But the room was full of people. How can you say you were the only one who heard her?"

"Because, I was the only one who heard her," I replied again, trying not to give anything away I didn't have to.

The attorney looked like he was ready to burst. I could tell he was wanting to attack me, and I got a glimpse of what it would be like when I was in court, but I'd rather have the intel on him now, so I was prepared for what court would look like in the future.

Finally, the man took a different turn, I guessed to try to unbalance me.

"How long have you known Suzie?" he asked.

"I've known Miss Fisher for just over four months," I replied.

"How did you meet?"

Mr. Edgerton chimed in at this point, "That's not relevant, sir. I object to that line of questioning."

"Your objection is noted, sir," the man said, then turned back to me. "You have to answer the question either way."

I looked at Mr. Edgerton for confirmation and he nodded curtly.

"We met through a friend," I replied.

"Who was your friend?"

"That is not any of your business either," I replied.

When I looked over at Mr. Edgerton, he smiled. "There is no reason why you can't tell him. It isn't relevant, but if you don't mind answering, please do."

"We were introduced by my brother and his boyfriend," I said.

The attorney got a disgusted look on his face then, and said, "Your brother is gay?"

I ignored the question, and looking over at Mr. Edgerton, he nodded approval.

"Well, that is certainly all I need to know," the attorney said.

"I have one more question for you, Mr. Freemont," Mr. Edgerton said.

"Did you ever meet Mr. McPeak before that day?" he asked.

"No, I'd never seen him before," I replied.

"Okay, that's all, then."

The other attorney paused, as if he had other questions, but I got up and gathered my things, heading out the door, before he could ask anything else. I suspected Edgerton was trying to egg on the other attorney, by showing he didn't ask if Suzie had ever discussed McPeak with me before. I wondered why he would give that away, but I didn't have to wait long, before I got my answer.

Mr. Edgerton led me to his office where Suzie was waiting. When I saw her, I had to hold back the tears. I had missed her more than I thought possible.

When we were done embracing, she pulled away. "I'm so sorry I had to hold you at a distance, but I needed to make sure we did this right. I can't let that son of a bitch win."

Mr. Edgerton looked over at me, and said, "Can you two have a seat? I want to discuss what happened today."

We did as he asked, and he sat on the edge of his desk facing us.

"Mr. McPeak has three attorneys, and they're all pit bulls. Today was all a show to let you get comfortable, but you need to be prepared. They will tear you apart during trial, or at least they will try to. I have a few cards up my sleeve as well."

"I did a little twist at the end, just to let him know we were onto him, but that won't help you much," he said. "Now, I'm pretty sure we'll get a settlement soon. It will be a bunch of garbage about Suzie staying silent, and there'll be threats of lawsuits if she says anything publicly.

"I don't need to tell you the entire case hinges on your testimony, Mr. Freemont, so if you aren't willing to go forward, you need to let us know now. Unfortunately, if this gets out, it could destroy Suzie's career, but if she's willing to make that sacrifice, I want to do everything I can for her to win."

I looked over at Suzie, who was ashen-faced. "Are you really willing to give up your career?" I asked.

She nodded. "You don't know what it's like to live in fear every day of your life, Indi. I can't allow him to have that much power over me—not again. If it means I no longer act, then yeah. If I don't have to feel like this any longer, then I'm willing to give it up."

I reached over, and hugged her. "Then, you need to know I'm behind you all the way. Of course, it helps knowing we'll be able to put that arrogant piece of shit in his place as well."

Suzie smiled at me, although it was a little sad. "Thank you, Indi."

I held her tighter. "Mr. Edgerton, is there any reason why we can't be together now?" I asked.

"No, the deposition should be enough to show the two of you didn't practice the testimony. As you said before, Suzie needs you." He smiled at her in a fatherly way.

"That's true," she said. "Indi, I do need you more than I would've admitted before all this happened. Can I stay with you tonight?"

"Yeah, I'd give about anything if you would."

Suzie and I left the attorney's office hand-in-hand. Her life had been turned upside down, and I couldn't do much about that, but I sure as hell could be there for her as she went through it. Fuck anyone who didn't approve.

# Suzie

After Indi's deposition, we sat at Vinnie's, staring at each other. Neither of us knew what to say. The situation was just too fucked up. How in the hell had that son of a bitch turned the cart on me? He tried to *rape* me. I escaped, then turned *him* in, and now he was suing *me*, not the other way around.

Indi held my hand, until the food was delivered. I'd never been so thankful to have a place that knew what I liked, because I really needed just to chill, and be with a man who was good and solid, and not think about things like ordering food.

When the meal came, however, I realized I wasn't hungry. My stomach was still in knots.

"Are you sure you're okay with testifying, Indi? If you aren't, I'm sure we can—"

Indi interrupted me before I could finish. "Suzie, stop that nonsense. Of course, I don't mind testifying. You are an amazing woman who has overcome so much. The fact that this horrible man is the reason you had to overcome it, makes me want to do serious damage to him. Since I can't do that without jeopardizing you *and* me, I'll settle with telling the truth about him."

"You do realize the press will eat you alive when they hear you're testifying. You'll be the fodder of as much humiliation as they can throw at you."

Indi laughed. "Suzie, I'm an agent. I'm clear how this will go down, and, yeah, it's going to suck. But it won't suck for me as much as it will for you. The press aren't the only ones who are going to come after you. His party, those who love him and support him, will call you every name in the book. They won't be able to defend his actions, so they will attack your character. They will also attack your show." Indi looked down then, like he'd possibly said too much.

I reached over and grabbed his hand. "Yeah, I already know that. I've told my director that when the shit hits the fan, they'll want to replace me with my understudy. I am not going to let the SOB undo me again, but I also need to fight to save my career, at least if that is possible…" I paused, then added, "That's why I need you to become my agent."

Indi sat back, stunned. He didn't say anything for a moment. "Suzie, are you sure? You probably need to stick with the agent you have while going through a crisis. Not that I'm not excited you would consider me, but everyone advises you don't jump ship when there's a hurricane."

I shook my head. "It isn't like I have much choice. My agent is a friend or follower of Eddie. She ended our contract the day I told her what happened."

"*What!?*" Indi exclaimed. "Marilyn Patterson dumped you at the front of a crisis. That's going to really hurt her when word gets around."

"How will word get around? I'm not going to say anything. Yeah, she fucked me over, but I'm not a big fan of vengeance."

Indi laughed, then said, "One of the first questions you'll be asked when the press finds out I'm your new agent, is why you let her go. Do you remember how quickly word got out about my client and her father?

How Joel told his director friend who told you? That's all going to come out sooner than later. Besides, when the shit hits the fan, are you prepared to lie for her?"

I stared at him for a moment. Choosing not to answer the part about my former agent, I asked, "So it's a yes, then?"

Indi continued laughing. "Suzie, you are something else. Of course, I'd be honored to be your agent. You're one of the best in the business, and if we play this right, it could boost your career instead of ending it."

I jumped out of my seat, ran over and leaped into Indi's lap. "You are the best boyfriend-agent in the whole world!" I planted a huge kiss on his lips.

Indi kissed me back, and it immediately went deeper. When we pulled apart, I realized we probably needed to get out of the public eye. If I were to guess, I was probably already being followed, and I didn't need to give them any fodder.

"Ready to go home?" I asked him.

"Yours or mine?" he asked.

"Yours. I'm sick of mine."

"I couldn't think of anything I'd like better," Indi said, and we called the server over to pack up our food.

If I hadn't had feelings for Indigo Freemont before, I sure did now. Not only had he agreed to testify for me, and stand up for me in court, he'd also agreed to take on the train wreck that was my career. Indi was the real deal. How the hell had I gotten so lucky?

# Indi

I immediately handed off my most time-consuming clients to a colleague that I knew would do a good job at managing them. One or two of the clients were upset, but when I told them I was taking on Suzie Fisher, they immediately offered their congratulations. Of course, they had no idea what kind of issues that entailed—at least not yet.

We pulled together our strategy team at the agency, and began troubleshooting how to deal with the inevitable fallout over the court case. In the end, we decided the best possible outcome would be to have Suzie lie low, until we knew for sure the case would make it to trial. If it didn't, then we'd spin any press with no comment. If it all blew up, then we'd have Suzie make a public announcement. She would certainly not like that, but we were all sure the show producers would require it anyway.

Suzie and I stayed together almost every night. I sensed she needed to have someone around, and I wanted to keep my eye out for any unforeseen dangers. Suzie was a formidable individual, and I had no doubt she could take care of herself, but no one could take the world on by themselves, and I'd be damned if she would ever have to as long as I was around.

Edgerton called it right. A week after the deposition, McPeak's firm offered a settlement. They would accept a non-disclosure in lieu of pursuing the lawsuit further. Suzie flat-out turned it down, and I guessed that would be the end of it, but Suzie threw them a twist. She asked Edgerton to countersue McPeak for emotional damages as well as any damages that occurred to her career as a result of this "frivolous lawsuit."

I was with Edgerton when Suzie announced she wanted to do this, which took both of us by surprise.

"Suzie," Mr. Edgerton began, "I don't believe this will ever go to trial. McPeak won't want this to go public, so after he learns you won't be intimidated, he'll probably back down. However, if you countersue, it's almost a guarantee that the case will go to court. Are you sure that's what you want?"

Suzie nodded. "I have been dealing with the fallout from Eddie McPeak since I was a teenager. I've allowed him to have too much power over my life, and I've allowed my fear to take center stage when it comes to other men and relationships. I didn't start this, but now that it's started, I have every intention of holding him accountable. They may have thought this would shut me up, but they made a mistake when they came after me. Mr. Edgerton, please file a countersuit immediately. It's time we fight fire with fire."

Suzie stood up then, and pulled me up with her. "When do you want me to come back to sign the paperwork?" she asked.

I hadn't seen this side of her, but I liked it. When she'd made up her mind, I doubted anything could stop her. Damn, if that didn't hit me in the gut as well. I was completely head over heels for Suzie Fisher!

"If you can stop by tomorrow afternoon, I'll have the paperwork ready for you to sign. I need to talk over strategy with my partners, and come up with what we believe will be the best approach for the countersuit. I can see you've made up your mind, but I need you to know, this will likely go public the minute we file the suit."

"I understand," she said as we walked toward the door. "Have your assistant contact me with the details." She turned and looked the old man in the eye. "Thank you, Mr. Edgerton. Your assistance means a lot to me. If I'm going to make this kind of sacrifice, let's make sure it counts."

Edgerton smiled slightly, and nodded. "Sure thing, Miss. Fisher."

***

As soon as we left the attorney's office, we found a little coffee shop around the corner to sit and decompress.

"Wow, Suzie, that was pretty extraordinary. What made you decide to take him on?"

Suzie sipped her coffee, quiet now, unlike she'd been in the attorney's office. "I'm so tired of being afraid, Indi. Since I got served, I've been in a whirlwind of what-ifs. What if it destroys my career, what if it destroys yours, what if this comes between us?" Suzie put her hand over mine then, tears forming in her eyes.

"I don't want to lose you. I don't want to lose my career either, but I can't run and hide from him. Everything in me says if I do, he'll be back again. Not only that, I'll have to see him running for office, and worse, what if he wins? Then that arrogant, horrible... bad man will be running our country. I can't let him have that much power over me, or anyone else if I can stop it. I need to stand up. If all else fails, I'm sure I can get a job as a drama coach. That was always my retirement plan anyway."

Suzie turned away, sadness all over her face. "I think I'd make a good coach, don't you?" she asked, without looking over at me.

"What I think is that you'll make an excellent coach—when you retire. But, you didn't hire the *best* agent in town just to throw in the towel. Time to put your Beta panties on and fight until the fight is over."

Suzie chuckled, then leaned over and kissed me before whispering in my ear, "Beta doesn't wear panties, silly."

How the hell, in the middle of *this* serious conversation, did she turn my brain to mush?

"Damn, Suzie," was all I got out before she cackled that amazing Broadway laugh across the coffee house, causing everyone close to turn. Most of them smiled when they realized who she was. We left and headed directly over to my house and spent the rest of the day making love.

# Suzie

Knowing there was going to be a whirlwind, and being prepared for it, were two different things. Days after we filed the countersuit, the press got wind of it. Even though the case was technically sealed, someone had either leaked it, or there was a snafu in the court filings. Everyone advised me to not look at the things being written, but I couldn't help it. It seemed like every tag line in the media started with my name.

Indi's agency immediately hired a publicist to manage the onslaught. She was a powerhouse of a woman from Los Angeles who had a lot of experience with the stars from Hollywood.

Many papers confused me with my character, and blatantly said I was the biggest slut in New York. One even used the name Beta instead of my own. I was pleased that those caused me to chuckle more than upset me. They would only bring more publicity to the show, and didn't do any real harm.

The ones that bothered me were the ones that painted Eddie as the victim. Stating that I had never really met him, but had told a crowd of people that he had raped me. There were too many details for a reporter to put together, indicating that Eddie or his defense team were behind these accusations. It was clear the leak *must* have come from him.

When I brought this up to Mr. Edgerton, he immediately filed a motion to gag any discussions with the press until the case was done. Eddie's team fought the order of course, stating that they needed to defend him in the public's eye, since he had an election coming up, likely before the case was done.

Edgerton brought the article in question up to the judge, and reiterated that the case had been sealed, due to a request from Mr. McPeak's legal team. It wasn't until after the countersuit was filed that this information was leaked to the press.

Eddie's team argued that they hadn't leaked it, but now that it was out, it was essential that he be able to defend himself.

The judge ended up agreeing to the gag order, but only in respect to the specifics of the case. If Eddie wanted to speak about being in court and denying the charges in public, that would be allowed.

"Two can play at that game," Edgerton said after leaving court. "Suzie, make sure you don't personally say anything in public, but you can have your agent or publicist make a statement, just have him or her run it by me first."

I agreed, and Indi immediately called a meeting between the publicist, whose name was Jules, and himself to discuss putting together a public statement.

Jules came to the meeting prepared. She put the statement she recommended on the table in front of us. "You need to come back strong, and you need to be angry with a mixture of grief."

"That won't be hard, because that's exactly how I'm feeling," I replied.

She smiled a sad, knowing smile. "I know, Suzie. I'm sorry, and our conversations are going to often sound like I'm not paying attention to the emotional elements of this for you, but the public has to be shown your reactions in a certain way, if you want them to sympathize with you."

I nodded. "I know. I didn't mean to be emotional about it, but as we go through this, we need to keep in mind that a lot of lives are wrapped up in this, not only mine and Indi's, but also my parents and brother. This could also negatively impact the show I'm in, as well as anyone who's had something similar happen. Letting the idiots play this off as all my fault, discounts their experiences too."

Jules agreed. "I promise, we will take all that into consideration, but at the moment, we need to turn the tide back toward McPeak and his attack dogs.

"I did a Google search before coming in today, and there were fifteen thousand links that had to do with this court case. That's significant for the short time it has been in the public's eye. Of those, I could only find three that shined a positive light on you, Suzie. We have to change that first.

"We can use the negativity to mount our response, simply by contracting the statements. I have a couple reporter friends I trust to take your official statement, and spin it so they make the arguments against him.

That way they aren't coming directly from you. This will spark a debate among the different contingencies.

"I can't reiterate enough how important it is for you to stay in the background. Today's politics are all about propaganda. Each side will make its own arguments, and each side will be disgustingly wrong. The courts will play out in their own way, and since the judge isn't going to gag the courtroom, everything you say or do will be public. That is when the speculation will be turned to fact.

"Meanwhile, you can expect your opponent to publicly bash you in every way possible. This is good, because if it's spun correctly, it will make you look more like the victim, and less like the perpetrator, which appears to be their game plan."

The public statement was simple:

*Since both parties of this case have been ordered by the judge not to disclose aspects of the trial, I will not divulge specifics in this statement.*

*What I will say, however, is that I strongly deny that anything I have said harmed Mr. McPeak in any way. This lawsuit was a complete surprise, and came about after spending only a few moments in Mr. McPeak's company.*

*Prior to seeing him at a party in New Haven, I hadn't seen Mr. McPeak since I was a teenager.*

*Both Mr. McPeak and I are going to have an opportunity to air our grievances in the Connecticut Court System, so I ask that everyone have patience with the legal process.*

Once Edgerton gave his approval, the statement was released. As Jules had predicted, the statement hit the public, and the different poles of opinion spun it the way they wished.

Luckily, the statement also had the effect of causing the debate to become more equitable. No longer was Eddie's victim spin on this the only one on the internet, rather, the women's groups, and the #MeToo movement took up the cause, and defended me against the other side's attacks.

What was remarkable was that I didn't really have to say or do anything to alter the discussion.

The week before the first day of trial, McPeak had a debate with his opponent, Aleah Pinkerton, a younger woman with a fiery disposition.

During the debate, she confronted McPeak on the allegations of attempted rape. Of course, he denied it, but she pulled out the police report from our case.

I could tell that Eddie was surprised she had that—as was I. I thought all those files would've been sealed, since he was underage, but apparently not. Eddie said that was all a misunderstanding.

When Pinkerton pushed him on what he meant by a misunderstanding, he became ruffled, and said, "The woman is lying."

After that, he refused to speak about it further, using the excuse that the judge had ordered him to remain silent about that, while his lawsuit against me was in process.

I had to give it to him. Eddie was a master at spinning the truth. The way he said it made it sound like it was my fault. Pinkerton, however, was clearly not convinced. She had a serious look of disgust on her face, and the camera zeroed in on her as he spoke.

The next question asked was to her, and it was an audience question. I strongly believe the question was planted, because there was no way she could've gotten a better platform to stand on. A young girl stood up, and asked his opponent what she would do if she were elected to protect the rights of women, and children from rape and sexual exploitation. Yes, she actually used that word.

The camera panned to Eddie as his opponent replied how every man, woman, and child had the right to say no. Eddie's face was mutinous. Seeing it caused an immediate flashback to right after the incident. I hadn't gone to the police station, but my mom and dad had, while my aunt stayed with me. When they came back, I heard my mom say to her sister, when they thought I wasn't in my room, that the boy had clearly felt entitled to what he had done, and was mutinous and angry. I realized he was doing the very same thing here, and my stomach turned as I wondered how many times he'd done this very thing to other women. Someone with that expression must feel entitled to any woman's body that he wanted.

The following morning, our publicist Jules called, and stated that Eddie's opponent had contacted her, and asked if we could plan a meeting. Jules highly recommended that I decline, as it would give fodder to the public debate that I was being political, and that could hurt my career. However, she said she would go in my place if I gave her permission, which of course, I did.

The afternoon following her meeting with Eddie's opponent, she texted me and said she needed to meet with Mr. Edgerton, Indi, and me. She had gotten some interesting information that would likely impact the case against me.

Edgerton wasn't available that day, or the next due to a conflict with his court schedule, but we met the following day early, since I had to be at a performance that night.

Jules had remained in New York after her meeting with the politician, which meant this was a big deal. She disclosed to us that there were three other victims who had approached her campaign after the debates. She said the women appeared credible.

Edgerton looked concerned, when he turned to me, and said, "We aren't trying McPeak for rape. He is suing *you* for slander. If we get these women involved, it could backfire on you. Really, you only need to prove you didn't accuse him of raping you."

He paced a bit around the room, then came back to the table we were sitting at.

"Jules, did Ms. Pinkerton say she was going to go public with these statements?" he asked.

"She didn't, no. From what I could gather from the tenor of the conversation, she would prefer they come out through the courts."

Mr. Edgerton nodded sagely, scratching his chin. "For once, this would be better if it comes out in the public. I don't think I could use them in the case, but I do think they could be used to discredit McPeak's character, if the information was already available."

Jules said, "I understand, and I agree."

She looked over at me, and said, "Suzie, if you aren't the only one on the firing line, it'll do a lot to support you as a victim of McPeak's actions, as well as help to prove that you are the victim of this lawsuit. We haven't done well explaining why you are countersuing him. This will help us spin that as you're seeking justice."

I said, "Which is truly the case."

"Jules," Mr. Edgerton said, "I highly recommend that you not become involved with Pinkerton directly. Remember, you can be called as a hostile witness against Suzie. If they think you are collaborating with their enemy, that could become an issue that we may have to defend in court."

"Agreed. I already thought about that, and if I'm seen at the campaign headquarters more than once, it won't help Suzie in the public eye either. I have friends in her party, though. I will meet with them, and let them know what we discussed."

We all agreed, and as we were about to leave, Edgerton asked me to hang back, so he could speak to me privately. So, I stayed while Jules and Indi went out.

When the door closed, Edgerton motioned for me to sit down. "Suzie, I've made some typical motions, as has McPeak's team. Court won't likely be much more than the discussion of those motions. What I wanted to discuss with you, though, is that you be prepared. We've already been warned, the courtroom is expected to be full of reporters.

"There are some basic rules I advise any of my clients when fighting both in court and in the public. You may not like them all, but I've learned over the years if you follow these, it'll make it a lot easier for all of us.

"First, you need to know McPeak's team may have put people in the crowd to get you to say something they can use. It's playing dirty, but it isn't uncommon. So, my first bit of advice is for you to remain friendly to the reporters. Smile when it is appropriate, and frown when it isn't. Let me handle the press. Even though they will be asking you questions directly, don't say a word.

"While you are standing next to me, you need to look sad and concerned. I wouldn't normally say that to a client, but as an actress, it wouldn't hurt for you to use your skills, because like it or not, the minute you show up in court, you will be on stage.

"Next, I don't think you'll be safe in public after the trial starts. McPeak isn't in a good spot, and he is going to fight dirty. When Blasey-Ford was under the microscope, she received numerous death threats. Although this isn't as big of a public case, I think it would be wise if you had security with you, especially before and after court. I also recommend you have it throughout the trial as well. Understood?"

I nodded, but my stomach was in a twisted knot. I'd never needed security, even though I was pretty well known in my role as Beta. I'd hoped I could avoid it for the length of my career, but I also knew he was probably correct. It only took one idiot, and everything would be over.

"Finally, there isn't anything I can do to make this process any less painful. It is what it is. You have to fight both in court as well as in the public's eye. However, that doesn't mean you can't enjoy the small victories. I doubt we'll get our motion to dismiss approved tomorrow, but I doubt they will get theirs to dismiss your countersuit either. *That* will be a big deal, because there has to be justification and potential damages for either to go through. I will be demonstrating to the courts tomorrow, just how much you have suffered since this began. I will be showing the slanderous articles, as well as the statement McPeak made in his debate. The truth is when he called you a liar, he slandered you, and that should be more than enough for us to justify your suit against him."

I nodded again. The legal crap was difficult for me to understand. It was beginning to feel more like a chess match than a genuine discussion about justice, but I trusted Edgerton knew his game. I left the conference room, feeling like I might puke.

Indi and Jules were waiting for me in Edgerton's lobby. We walked out together, and Jules asked us to come with her to a restaurant she knew just around the corner. I had to decline, since I would have to get dressed and to the theater in enough time to warm up.

"I understand," she said. "But, I would like to see you before I fly back to LA. What's your schedule like tomorrow morning?"

I sighed, realizing that I'd miss my late morning sleep-in and my workout with Indi. I'd come to really depend on those over the past few weeks. We didn't say much as we worked out, but having him there with me always lifted my spirits.

"Sure, but not until after 10 a.m. I'm going to need to sleep a full eight hours tonight. If I don't, it could send me down an unhealthy stress cycle. Those are ugly when they get in full swing."

Jules nodded, and we went our separate ways. Indi leaned down to kiss me, before heading to work, and I pulled him into a hug. "Indi, thanks for being here for me. It means more to me than you know. I don't think

I'd be able to deal with the stress of the public, performing, and court if I didn't have you by my side."

I felt the tears behind my eyes and tried to blink them back.

"I know, Suzie. It's my pleasure, though. Keep up your spirits, and we'll get through this, I promise."

I nodded into his chest, and then, even though I really didn't want to, I let him go. "I'm going to stay at my apartment tonight, since it's closer to the theater. I really need to get a good night's sleep. I feel like I'm running on fumes here."

Indi looked like he was going to disagree, but nodded instead. "You call me if you change your mind, though, okay?" he asked.

I said okay and kissed him, before I turned to run toward the subway. I had just enough time to get home, get dressed, and get to the theater to warm up.

# Indi

I was concerned about Suzie going home alone. I'd been worried since her name flashed across the political screen, but so far, nothing seemed too concerning. Suzie had spent most nights with me anyway, which was beyond amazing.

I had changed my schedule at work to be more accommodating to hers, which also worked for my other clients, considering they all tended to have similar schedules. We'd usually lie in bed until late, then wake up making love.

We'd both dress and head to the gym, and then shower and be on our way.

We had quickly fallen into a relationship-like routine, and I loved it. Clay and Denim spent most nights at our house as well, and when Suzie wasn't working, we would end up eating together, and enjoying the camaraderie of our little family.

As it turned out, my concern was justified. I got her frantic call around 1 a.m. She said her apartment had been broken into, and someone had ripped up a bunch of her clothes and written "Sluts Must Die" and "Deuteronomy 22" on her wall.

Suzie was waiting for me in her neighbors' flat while the police walked through her apartment. She seemed too calm to me, but when I approached her for a hug, she pulled away, then apologized, saying she needed a little space while she processed things.

I just nodded. How much more could this woman handle?

Before the cops left, the one in charge, a tall husky blonde woman, told Suzie she really needed to have someone with her at all times. According to the woman, this was personal. Clothes weren't typically ripped apart during a robbery. And then there was the threat spray painted on her wall. I agreed with the detective. Now that Suzie was being threatened, it was time to step up our game. I probably should've already pushed her, as her agent, if not as her boyfriend. Suzie needed protection. Simple as that.

After they left, I walked behind Suzie as she went through her things. She cried the entire time. Her clothes were strewn all over the apartment, many of them torn or cut with a knife. There were knife marks slicing through her sofa and side chair as well. The kitchen was mostly untouched. Apparently, the intruder had focused more on the bedroom and living room.

"Suzie, I don't want to push," I said. "But I'd feel a lot better if you were with me tonight. If you want me to, I can take tomorrow off and help you put this back together." I waved my hand toward the mess.

Suzie agreed. I could see her spirit had drained out of her. There wasn't much that affected this powerful woman, but apparently, Eddie McPeak, and whoever had done this in his name were the exception.

Suzie came over and put her head on my shoulder. "Thank you for being here," she said quietly as she let me hold her. We stood that way for a moment before she pulled away, and said, "Let's go to your place, I'll deal with this later. Right now, I just want to focus on you and me, and forget all this ugliness for a while."

When we got back to my place, and were cuddled up in bed, I lay staring up at the ceiling for a long time. I couldn't tell if Suzie was asleep or not, but it felt good to have her in my arms as she was processing all that had happened to her.

The next day, I called my friend who ran a security company for many of the stars on Broadway. He and I had worked together in the past, and I wanted to have him available if Suzie agreed to my plan.

I knew this wasn't something she'd want, which was why I'd dropped the ball by not suggesting it earlier. As I could've predicted, she hated the idea.

"I don't want some man following me around night and day," she argued.

"I know, Suzie, and that's why I talked to my friend Peter, who runs a security firm. I trust him, and he has a couple women on staff that he thinks would be perfect for you."

Suzie looked at me, astonished. "Really? You aren't going to argue for some stupid beefed-up man on steroids?"

I looked down at my body, and said, "Not all of us are steroid ridden," which caused her to chuckle.

"I'm sorry, Indi," she said. "I'm just surprised you aren't more..."

I could tell she was at a loss for words, so I said it for her. "You're surprised I'm not a male chauvinist pig?"

Suzie sighed. "I'm sorry," she said again. "This has my head all fucked up. I guess I need to thank you, because if you weren't the amazing man you are, I would be going full-out man-hater at this point."

I nodded in agreement. "Yeah, and for good reason, but Honey, don't forget we aren't all that way. I'm here for you, and I know having a bunch of men you don't know hanging all over you won't work. So, I think these women might be perfect, and if you don't like them, he did say a few of his guys were out of the closet..."

She laughed out loud for the first time in a long while. "You're too good at this," she said. "I want the gay guys and the women on my detail. Yeah, I agree." She sat down hard on my sofa. "I don't like it, but I agree."

"I know, Baby. I know you don't like it." Then I went over and sat next to her. "Let's call Peter and see if he can set up a time for you to meet the team he would put on your detail. Then, we can make plans about how to incorporate them into your life."

She sighed again, and leaned over into me. "I appreciate all this, but I plan to bitch about it as often as I can. I hope whomever this Peter guy has picked out is prepared for that."

I chuckled. "These people have dealt with much more temperamental prima donnas than you'll ever be. That I can promise!"

We both laughed at that. The performance industry was nothing if not full of drama queens.

# Suzie

earning to tolerate having anyone in my space twenty-four seven was a challenge. The break-in at my apartment, however, convinced me I shouldn't try to handle this on my own.

I guessed part of me lost what little innocence I had left that night. I had convinced myself that I was safe, that I had built my body up enough that I could protect myself against a perpetrator, or that in a situation where I was in danger, I'd be in a public-enough environment that I could get help. But, I kept thinking, what if I'd been alone in that apartment, what if my brother had been visiting, or even if Indi had been spending the night.

A bad guy with a knife or a gun could do even the biggest and strongest in.

So, I agreed to the protection, but I didn't have to like it.

I made a strong effort to be kind to my bodyguards. I even tried talking them into having a cup of coffee with me, or in participating in what I was doing, but they always declined.

"No, Miss Fisher, I need to stay focused," they'd always say.

I knew they were right, but if they could've been more friendly, maybe this would've been easier.

Renee and Kiesha were both great women, and I hoped when this was all over, we could become friends, or at least workout partners. They would accompany me to my morning workout, and stay with me through the entire routine. From time to time, I'd even threaten to force them to spot me, just to annoy them, which they took in good humor. I was thankful for that, because I knew for a fact if I'd been in their situation, I wouldn't have. One of the women was with me throughout my day, and was usually replaced by Les, who was my primary nighttime bodyguard.

Les was a six-foot-four beefcake, who stood a whole inch taller than Indi. He was a total gushing sweetheart beneath his monster exterior. I initially threatened to fix him up with one of my friends, but he quickly let me know he was happily married, and he and his husband had two adorable boys they were raising.

Almost every night I'd rile Indi up by threatening to run away with Les. Les would just laugh, and tell me my plumbing wasn't quite the right fit, then he'd pull out his phone, and show us the most current pictures of his *way* too adorable family. It was so awesome to see this level of love. I even caught Indi smiling as the big man gushed over his little boys, or waxed romantic about his husband.

When Les was off, there were three other men who took his place. I didn't get very close to any of them, but most of them worked out at the gym where Indi and I went. Since Indi knew them at least on that level, I trusted we were okay in their hands.

My parents, along with Aiden and his husband, Devin, showed up to be with me at court. This wasn't something they'd told me they were going to do. In fact, they deliberately didn't tell me, knowing I'd have tried to talk them out of it.

The good news was, having them there distracted me, and kept me from thinking about court. Indi and my dad were like peas in a pod. Even Aiden's new man, Devin, seemed to enjoy having Indi around.

The court day came and went, and Eddie was his typical arrogant self. My attorney had motioned the courts to dismiss based on the grounds that the lawsuit was frivolous. Of course, Eddie's attorneys argued that my countersuit was the only frivolous one, and we all ended up losing our motions, which Edgerton told me was completely expected.

Expected it might be, but that didn't make it any less infuriating. Edgerton smoothed my feathers, and said we had an excellent case. Dalton, Kristina and Kristina's mom had agreed to testify that they were in the room where Eddie and I saw each other, and they didn't hear anything. I remembered they all three were in various places around the room when Eddie came in and gave his disgusting speech. Dalton was probably too far away to be a reliable witness, since he was almost in the kitchen, and I didn't remember exactly where Kristina or her mother were when he confronted me.

Edgerton said he had other sworn affidavits if those were needed from several other parties in the room. Luckily, most of Eddie's fans were in the den behind the kitchen. Dalton's parents were the only ones in the room when Eddie and I talked, but neither of their names appeared on the approved witness list. In truth, that was appropriate, because both of them were at the door, and greeted Eddie when he came in. They stood next to him through his speech, and then ventured toward Dalton after Eddie finished speaking.

I hadn't remembered this, but Indi had. I was guessing Dalton also remembered this, and that was why they didn't agree to testify against me.

Other than that, Eddie's girlfriend, who was on the witness list, was the only other person in the room who could say she was close enough to hear. However, when Eddie came up to me, I'd noticed that she had turned toward the table to peruse the food. Indi had barely heard me, and he was standing right next to me when I spoke, so there was no way she could've overheard our conversation either. Unfortunately, that didn't mean she wouldn't lie for him.

Edgerton sent us on our way, assuring us all was well in hand, and that he'd call us if he needed us for any reason.

***

The day after court, someone released a photo of my apartment with the writing on the wall to the press. It immediately swept across social media, and Jules called me early on the morning it hit to warn me.

"You need to be ready, because this is going to hit like a ton of bricks," she told me.

"Can you tell who put this out first?" I asked.

"Yes and no. It appears to have started with an obscure newspaper out of North Carolina. I'm not sure why they were interested in a political piece from Connecticut, but that's where the first article appears to have come from.

"Of course, mainstream programs, have grabbed it and are coating television and the internet with it."

"What are the friendly news outlets saying?" I asked.

"Not much. They don't seem to have gotten ahold of it yet, but you can bet they will. The scripture reference, if nothing else, will cause a bit of a stir."

I hadn't even considered the scripture reference until then. The truth was, I just figured this was a wigged-out crazy person, and New York had plenty of people yelling scripture verses at you as you walked along the streets, or even into the subways. So, I just sort of forgot to look that up.

"Um," I said to Jules, "I kind of forgot to look up the scripture. What's it about?"

Jules was silent for a moment. "Honey," she said, using an endearment for the first time since I'd met her. "It's really ugly."

"Well, that's okay, just tell me. It can't be worse than having someone break into your home and cut your clothes up with a knife," I told her.

"Okay, I don't have it memorized, but basically it says if a woman doesn't scream loud enough when she is being raped, the rape is her fault."

I was wrong. This was worse than having my apartment and clothing trashed. I couldn't speak for a moment, feeling like the breath had been knocked out of me.

When I was finally able to catch my breath, I wheezed out, "The Bible actually says that?"

"Apparently," Jules said, her voice dry. "I'm really sorry I'm the one to break that to you, but there's going to be a lot of negative press as well as public reaction to this when it gets out. You have to be ready, because this will give way too many crazies all the ammunition they need to blame this whole thing on you. And they *are going* to blame it on you."

Again, I was struck with silence, before I was able to ask, "Who... who is going to blame me?"

Jules sighed, "His supporters, Suzie. They're so determined to fight, and hate anyone not of their political persuasion that they will take his side, and justify his actions—whatever's necessary to get him the win."

"It's so sick, though," I whined.

"Yeah, it is," Jules agreed. "And there are thousands of victims who are going to read that crap, so you need to be strong. You can't let this get to you—at least not in the public's eye. I'm so sorry you're having to endure this, but in the long run, it's going to be good for you. It's going to show the world just how horrible this has been for you."

All I could do was sigh, and try to keep myself from vomiting. "I'll work on it, Jules. Let me know if I need to make another statement or anything, okay?"

"Okay," she said, and hung up.

I sat down on Indi's sofa and stared at the wall. I was numb. Did the Bible really say that? Surely not, no one could believe rape could be the fault of the victim. Even thinking that, I knew I was wrong. Too many victims had been blamed for being too drunk, or dressing too sexy, or any number of irrelevant excuses to justify the perpetrator's actions. I realized after I thought this, the numbness was gone, and instead of tears, the only emotion I felt was rage.

***

The media storm only lasted a few days before something else caught their attention, but the damage had been done. Horrible, nasty, and hateful things had been said about me and other victims of rape or sexual assault.

It was countered by reasonable people, but the shock factor of the nasties couldn't be outdone.

Several weeks after court, we got a call from Edgerton.

"Are you available to come to the courtroom if you are needed this afternoon?" he asked.

"Of course," I replied, confused.

Edgerton, catching the confusion, laughed and said, "Mr. McPeak has been arrested."

"What?" I asked in astonishment. "What for?"

Edgerton chuckled again, but this time in a conspiratorial way. "He was arrested for hiring the man who broke into your apartment."

"Fuck," I said, before realizing I was talking to my attorney.

"Exactly my thought," he said. "I'm making a new motion to dismiss his case based on this new information. He's in jail, so this is the perfect time to force the issue in front of the judge."

"Can you prove he did it?" I asked.

"Not exactly, but I don't really need to. I have the public information about the arrest, as well as the forms New York had to fill out to have him extradited here from Connecticut."

"Fuck," I said again, causing Edgerton to chuckle anew.

"I plan to submit the motion as soon as we're done talking, but I wanted to ensure you can be with me if we're called into court."

"Yeah, I'm available."

"I need Indi too. It's possible the judge will want to hear from him. Can he make it also?"

I put Edgerton on hold, and went up to the bedroom to find Indi, who was getting ready to leave for work. After I told him what had happened, he said he'd find a way to go with us if needed.

When I told Edgerton, the man was ecstatic. "Okay, stay close to your phones. I'll let you know what happens."

As it was, we never had a chance to meet Edgerton at the courthouse. Eddie's attorney contacted him less than an hour after he had filed the motion. Edgerton asked us to meet him at his office instead, and presented us with Eddie's conditions to drop the case. Of course, he wanted to save face and asked that I not press charges against him. If I agreed to this, he'd pay me one million dollars to settle my counter suit, and drop his slander case against me.

Of course, this was a laugh. Instead, I asked Edgerton to send this to his attorney:

He would pay for my damages, attorney fees and security expenses incurred thus far, and for another sixty days as that was appropriate for dragging my name through the mud, and I would agree to drop the suit.

He would make a public apology for dragging me through the mud, and for attempting to rape me when we were kids.

He would drop out of the election and agree never to run for public office, or accept a public position such as prosecutor, public defender or judge.

He would agree to spend at least sixty days in jail for the damages to my apartment, and for trying to scare me through intimidation or threatening my life.

Edgerton said the New York criminal courts would have to agree to the last part, but he'd get in touch with the prosecutor before he went any further. Later, the prosecutor said he'd allow this plea deal if Eddie pleaded guilty, and agreed to six months in county jail... sixty days wasn't enough, he said.

It took about a week before Edgerton got back to us. Eddie had agreed to all my requirements, except for two. He wouldn't pay the entire amount we requested, and he refused to admit he tried to rape me. Instead, his attorney changed the language to:

*He would make a public apology for dragging my name through the mud, and for any other damages this case had caused.*

I had spent more than what Eddie had offered to pay for damages due to the twenty-four-hour security, Indi's company's expenses and my publicist's costs, as well as other expenses related to this whole fiasco, but if it ended this, I'd be more than happy to eat the rest of the costs. Eddie might not be out and out admitting he tried to rape me, but the public apology all but announced that anyway—at least to anyone who didn't have an ulterior motive.

I guessed that once he left politics, that would all slip away too. People were arguing for him more because of their desire to win the seat he was running for, than a personal affinity for him. He'd see that all too soon once all this went through.

I met with Eddie's prosecutor before he signed the final documents to submit Eddie's plea deal to the courts. I was able to learn that Eddie's friend, the guy who he'd hired to wreck my apartment, had leaked the case to the small newspaper in North Carolina. It only took a bit of persuasion for the paper to release who he was, since they didn't have the revenue to deal with a huge fight in the courts, and, of course, the idiot hadn't signed anything about keeping his name a secret, so they were pretty much free to tell the police who he was.

Once they arrested the man, he immediately made a deal to disclose who had hired him, if it would keep him from going back to jail.

When Eddie moved away all those years ago, he and the perp had gone to high school together, and although they really hadn't kept in touch, when he was released for good behavior, Eddie approached him and agreed to pay him to break in and trash my apartment, as well as write the threatening statement.

The idea to sell the picture to the press had been all his idea, though, and luckily that ended up blowing the case open.

Jules contacted me shortly after the deal was agreed upon, and the details of the agreement were disclosed to the press.

"Would you like to make a public appearance at a conference to end sexual abuse against women and exploited children?" she asked.

At first, I wasn't sure, and I put her off, so I'd have time to think about it.

Indi listened as I worked through it all, and in the end, I decided, after all the pain I'd been through as a result of Eddie McPeak, I'd like to be able to speak out in public about the horror it had been for me, my family, and even Indi and my other friends.

***

The conference was full, which Jules told me had as much to do with my speaking as anything. I was still a hot topic in the press, and my being there brought good publicity to the event.

I had spent endless hours poring over my speech, hoping that what I wrote would express all the emotions and turmoil we had undergone throughout the process.

Strangely, when I stood up to speak, I wasn't nervous at all. Instead, I had a lightness to me I hadn't felt since... well, probably since I was a teenager.

I stepped up to the microphone with a burning confidence. The crowd met me with expectation, but in each of the mostly women's faces I saw understanding, and kindness.

*"Thank you for having me. Let me begin by saying, I didn't ask to be placed in a political debate. Unfortunately for me, for my friends, and family, as well as the company I work for, I was thrown into all of this when Mr. Edward McPeak attempted to silence me with a lawsuit. I'm no politician. I have always made a distinct effort to keep my politics to myself, and that's because I have family and friends who I respect on both sides of the political line.*

*"As you know, Mr. McPeak not only wielded a civil lawsuit as a weapon to shut me up, but he has also pleaded guilty to hiring an ex-con friend of his to break into my apartment,*

*destroy my belongings, and spray paint a threat, which most of you have seen in the media. The scripture that Mr. McPeak and his friend chose was an obscure passage that essentially says a woman who doesn't scream loud enough is guilty of the rape herself.*

"Like politics, I'm not here to debate religion or scripture. I'm just as unqualified to discuss that as I am the former. What I do know, and will speak about with no trepidation is that rape is never the fault of the victim. No one can dress too sexy, or be too flirty, or whatever excuse a rapist may use to justify taking advantage of someone without expressed consent.

"I have to admit that I truly don't know if circumstances had been different, whether I would've been brave enough to face my perpetrator had he not forced my hand. In that way, maybe I should be thankful it worked out like it did, because sometimes we can be our bravest when our back is up against a wall.

*"We now know the death threat made against me was a ruse, and another ploy to silence me. But, for many victims that death threat is all too real. We have all witnessed brave women who have come forward and exposed their perpetrator, only to have their own names trashed in the media.*

*"Many women, men, and children have accused their perpetrator, only to see police forces, family, communities, and even court systems turn against them. It is a sad reality, but even in America, it isn't always safe for someone to expose their perpetrator.*

*"For that reason, I firmly believe the decision of exposing a perpetrator must remain at the sole discretion of the victim. Instead of making victims who have chosen to stay silent wrong or bad, as many people have, I would implore anyone who knows of a person who has experienced these horrors, to rally around them, and ensure they have the necessary programs and support to recover as best they can.*

"We often think the worst thing that can happen to a person is physical violence. Yes, it can be detrimental and often it can lead to death, but the body can recover from that. However, violence that causes mental stress isn't as easily overcome.

"Rape victims, victims of child sexual abuse, and victims of most, if not all, sexual assaults suffer from the most enduring of mental anguish. This is why I believe sexual assault is a crime against the soul.

"For me, I have suffered many years where I have not allowed people to get close— especially men. For this reason, I have lost many years of healthy relationship development that most other people experience early on. I'm lucky, because I have found someone who is strong enough, and kind enough, to allow me to learn to trust him. For that, I will always be thankful.

"As we all move forward from this horrible set of events, let's remember that we need to listen to those who say they have been sexually *assaulted. If you are a victim, I urge you to seek and find those who can provide safe, judgement-free assistance to overcome your abuse.*

*"Very often the rejection that victims experience from family and friends can be as detrimental as the assault itself. If your family member or friend confides in you that they have been abused, I urge you to pause before you decide that the person is lying. Even when you are afraid, or confused, stand with your friend or family member. Allow the truth to come out before you cast any judgement.*

*"As a country and a society, we must overcome the temptation to ignore or belittle victims when they come forward. Law enforcement, attorneys, and judges must be screened to ensure they can respect these victims. Basic provisions can be set in place within all those organizations, to ensure sexual assault victims aren't discriminated against before they have had a chance to plead their case.*

"I repeat. I am not a politician, or a religious scholar. I am a woman who has been victimized by sexual assault. I speak as an expert only on how that has influenced me, and how I've seen the same, or worse, influence others.

"We have the power to make a difference in this world. Let's come together for change on that grand scale, but also to make the world just a bit safer and more supportive for those who are at risk of sexual assault or have already experienced it.

"Thank you."

# Indi

There was a thunder of applause that echoed throughout the room when Suzie finished speaking, and it lasted for well over five minutes as Suzie stood on the stage, not as the indignant Beta she usually played, but as the humble, beautiful, and powerful woman I'd come to know and love.

Realizing I was in love with Suzie wasn't a shock to me. I'd been coming to that conclusion since I'd first met her, but watching her on that stage, facing all her scariest demons, had convinced me if I lived to be a thousand years old, I'd never meet a woman who was quite as strong as her.

Suzie had turned to me during her speech, and winked when she said she'd found someone who supported her, but I wondered if she knew how much she had done for me in return. I could give as passionate a speech about all that she did to make my life better, more complete, easier, and more fun to live.

That night, I held Suzie while we lay in the big hotel bed. "You know I'm totally in love with you, don't you?"

Suzie pulled away and looked me in the eyes. "I didn't know for sure, until you just told me."

"Well, Suzie, I've never felt like this about anyone else, and I can't imagine I ever will again. You make my life shine in a way I never thought possible. My heart stops for a few seconds every time I see you after we've been apart. I think about you all the time, even when we're lying next to each other. I adore your incredible intellect, and I obsess over your incredible talent, and insanely hot body. You are the complete package. So, if that doesn't equate to love, I don't know what does."

Suzie had been listening to me as I rambled on, then she laid her head on my chest again, and waited a moment before she replied. Eventually, in a small voice, she said, "I don't think the word 'love' is enough for how I feel about you, Indi. You stood by me, helped me find my sexuality, and loved me through my trauma and fear." She pulled away again and looked at me. "Indi, not only do you complete me, but you complement me... so, yeah, I love you too, but so much more than that."

She leaned up and kissed me then, and I felt the tear that had slipped down her face wet our joined lips.

When we pulled apart, I reached up to wipe the tear streak with my thumb. "Why are you crying?" I asked.

She chuckled. "Because this is an amazing gift—a miracle I never dreamed could happen."

I sighed. "Then, you won't be too surprised that I bought you a ring?"

Suzie's eyes widened, and she asked, "What...? *A what?*"

I laughed, crawled out of bed, and grabbed my pants off the floor to pull the ring box out of my pocket. I knelt next to the bed, grabbing Suzie's hand in mine, and while both of us were naked as the day we were born, said, "Suzie, it will make me so happy that I will be hysterically crazy for the rest of my life, if you'll agree to marry me."

Suzie grabbed the ring out of my hand, and slipped it on her finger, while jumping up and down on the bed. I couldn't help laughing at the typical Suzie response to the proposal.

I stood up, and when she had calmed down, and stopped squealing long enough for me to be heard, I said, "Well, is that a yes?"

Suzie flung herself off the bed and into my arms, and after laying one of the most passionate kisses I'd ever experienced on my lips, she drew back, then in a very sexy voice, said, "Oh, yeah! That is totally a yes!"

***

There are things that happen in life you never forget, and for me it was that night with Suzie, standing on that stage, hurt, but strong, speaking against what happened to her, but also to the millions of victims of similar assaults, and then our confession of love and our engagement. I knew that night would be forever etched into my mind.

Suzie Fisher Freemont would forever have my heart and soul, and thank God she agreed to have them.

# LOVE BY CHANCE

Blake Allwood

# Martin

I woke to the smell of onions and garlic frying. That was the most luscious smell in the world. I leaned up, stretching to see who was putting such an amazing aroma into the world. When I saw Elian cooking, both my heart and my groin lurched a bit. There were fewer things sexier to me than a hot man cooking in his kitchen.

Elian apparently knew what he was doing. It was clear that his sister had a knack for cooking, but I'd assumed Elian didn't. I self-reflected, realizing maybe I didn't think a man could be both business-minded and have the artistic techniques to create a good meal. Despite my prejudice against the businessman, the smells of onion and garlic certainly were a step in the right direction, and even if the food wasn't very good, the beautiful man was definitely good enough to eat.

*Crap!* I swore in my head, catching myself thinking of Elian as beautiful. Okay, truth be told, he was sexy as hell, but I quickly stamped my thoughts down. *No need going there. I'm spending the night alone with this man tonight, and we have an agreement to keep things business and platonic. Remember, platonic,* I reminded myself.

I stood up and walked into the kitchen. Elian looked over and flashed me that gorgeous smile of his. "I hope you're getting hungry. I decided to cook for you myself tonight instead of parading you through the city. Hopefully, you'll go easy on me since I'm not a pro like my sister is." He turned to put the marinated beef into the pan with the garlic and onions.

"I never complain when a man cooks for me. It is one of my favorite sights in the world. I'd rather see that than a stripper," I said with a self-conscious laugh.

Elian cocked an eyebrow at me, then hummed a stripping song, pretending to strip and flip the meat all at the same time.

"You are a goof," I said, teasing him. But the silly act had done more than a little to turn me on. Had things been different, I was almost sure poor Elian would have burned his meal after I did some of the things I was imagining to his body... things that involved him continuing with that sexy little dance.

I shook my head and turned to go back to the living room, giving myself time to clear the thoughts of bedding Elian out of my mind. As I turned, I asked, "So, what was the outcome of your meeting?"

Elian shook his head. "The bartender was inherited from the previous owner. In fact, I think they were having an affair. When the previous owner sold to me, she broke it off with him. Apparently, he's been using his position at the bar to get even with me. At least that is how he put it before he threw the bar towel at me and stomped out yelling he quit."

"He was deliberately sabotaging you?" I asked.

"It appears so," Elian replied. "Too bad, too, because he came highly recommended, and when he served *me* a drink, they were always top-notch."

"What are you going to do?" I asked.

"The manager has called in a favor from a man she used to work with. He is going to cover until we can find a bartender who doesn't want to chase off all our customers."

"I'm sorry that happened," I sighed.

"I'm just glad I had you come out this weekend. If we can fix this fast enough, I think we will save our bar business. I am going to be comping a lot of drinks for the next few weeks to build back our reputation," Elian sighed.

I nodded. "I think giving away a few good drinks to your repeat customers is a very good idea. Don't be surprised, though, if you have several people decline. You may need to make sure your wait staff is telling everyone you have a new barkeep. In fact, that could be the excuse for offering a free drink."

"Clever," Elian replied thoughtfully.

I yawned big and raised my arms over my head, causing my stomach to show under my shirt. When I glanced back at Elian, his face had gone from platonic to something very, *very* different.

"Um, where do you work out at?" he stammered.

I looked at him and, with a cocked eyebrow, asked, "Where did that come from?"

Elian blushed. "I noticed your abs when you were yawning," he replied. His face continued to turn a darker red from the awkward question.

I was enjoying the effect my stomach was having on Elian. The man seemed unflappable, but a little skin seemed to completely undo him. Yet, watching the man's reaction caused something to snap inside me as well. I'd been resisting my urge to kiss this guy since he'd showed up this morning, and his flustered awkwardness was the last straw.

I walked over to where he was cooking. Elian watched me with ever-widening eyes. I lifted my shirt over my abs, and then took it completely off. "I've been working out. All that restaurant food was going to turn me into a slob. What do you think?"

Elian gulped, and I chuckled low in my throat. "So, when is dinner going to be done?" I whispered in his ear.

"Um," was all Elian was able to get out, then he swallowed hard enough for me to hear.

"What?" I decided to play coy. "I just wanted to show you how I like to work out."

Again, Elian stammered but flipped off the heat under the pan. I laughed again, enjoying seeing this guy turned to mush over my body. I reached over and put my shirt back on, then leaned into Elian and kissed him square on the mouth.

"It is good to see you are as turned on by me as I am by you," I said, "but that doesn't mean we're going to do anything, Elian Whitman."

As I turned to leave, Elian spun me back around and kissed me deep and hard. This time, there was no civil peck; the kiss Elian gave possessed all the angst between us these past weeks. If I was going to pull back, it was going to have to be soon because Elian had just lifted the kiss to another level: tongue, saliva, and pure sexuality rolled into me like a storm surge in a category five hurricane.

Within an instant, my shirt was back off, and Elian's came off shortly after. We crossed the room, our kisses growing more passionate and desperate. Elian pushed me onto the sofa, and began assaulting my neck, then chest, and paused when he got to my nipples to nip ever so slightly. This was going to be raw sexuality, and Elian wasn't holding anything back.

Deep in the recesses of my mind, I could hear a faint cry from the part of my brain that told me to watch out—not to get close to a man again. *Especially this man, keep him at bay.* But instead of listening to that voice—which was just a little too easy to ignore—I responded to the need that Elian poured onto me.

***

To purchase Love By Chance, go to
*blakeallwood.com/booklink/2036661*

*****

To stay up to date on all of Blake's new releases, join his mailing list at:
*blakeallwood.com*

***